Don't Haunt Ghosts
Jeni Conrad

This book is dedicated to Tara Wine-Queen, a powerhouse of a
woman with a smile almost as beautiful as her heart.

Author's Note

As a teacher who has dealt with teens for many years, not to mention was once one herself, I wanted to bring up an issue in this series that many people struggle with. But for some, reading about it may be uncomfortable or even triggering. This story contains themes of an eating disorder. I am not trying to promote it or glamorize it in any way but rather trying to highlight the struggle a person might have with it and how damaging it can be. The issue does get resolved, but it takes several books to do so. If you or anyone you know struggles with an eating disorder, there is help. https://www.edreferral.com/

Contents

Chapter 1

My mom won't let us talk about it and any time I bring it up, she glares at me and changes the subject. I suppose I can't blame her—talking about her own mother's death has got to be uncomfortable at the least and severely painful at the most. It's not like I want to bring her pain, but it would be nice to talk about what only I saw that night.

Even though I was four at the time, some of the moments are clearly set in my memory while other moments are faded and distorted. Perhaps my mind has conveniently forgotten the more terrifying aspects to protect myself from the trauma and pain.

I was at Grandma Carey's house while she babysat me. Don't ask me where my parents were, probably on a date or something, but it wasn't like my younger, carefree self to pay attention to things like that. Trina, my sister who is fifteen months older than me, was at her piano lessons, and I do remember that because I might have been jealous that she got to take lessons. Not because I had the desire to play the piano or anything. Mostly, I just wanted to earn stickers when completing a song or get random lollipops like she'd get.

I might not have been so jealous if she'd shared once in a while.

But I digress.

As was our tradition when it was just Gran and me, we were in the kitchen making baby pancakes (they're like regular pancakes, but you make them small so they're more fun to eat, and I swear they taste better), when a knock sounded at the door.

Gran's eyebrows furrowed deeply. "I wonder who that could be. Stay here and don't touch the hot pan."

She left me in the kitchen and while I couldn't see who was at the door, I was able to hear the conversation. At first, I didn't pay much attention to it. I was too busy stirring the pancake batter, my job when we made pancakes, and I loved watching the clumps slop together.

Then they started yelling, and it was harder to ignore.

"Where is it? I know you have it!" A woman's voice sounded all the way from the front room, into the kitchen, and over the sizzle of the griddle.

"I don't know what you're talking about." My gran's voice was quiet, but strong and steady.

"Don't lie. You've got to have it, and if you won't help me, then I need it. You have no idea how important this is! I could be dead if I don't get to talk to him!"

"Then I guess you would be able to talk to him as much as you want."

I had no idea what they were arguing about, and I'm still clueless eleven years later. What I do know, however, is that the lady was mad, and she was going to get what she wanted, no matter what.

A large crash and shuffling sounds finally drew me away from the counter. Carefully, I stepped off the chair Gran had pulled up for me to stand on, and paused, unsure if I should go find out what was happening. Something inside was warning me to stay away.

"You're not going to find it here! Stop breaking my stuff!" Gran yelled above the chaos.

"If I can't have what I want, then you can't either!" Another shattering crash rumbled the floorboards.

This is where my mind gets fuzzy, but I'll try my best to tell the story.

Before I could go into the front room, another person was there. A man, I'm sure of that, at least. He was tall and he bent down so I could see him. I do remember his smile was bright and even though I was scared, he made me feel at ease. I also remember how he smelled—a frosty, minty scent that reminded me of a cozy winter morning.

"Hey, little bit. Something is happening and I need to go help your grandma, but it's also important that you stay hidden, okay?"

I nodded, probably with wide, scared brown eyes.

"It's okay, sweetie. Just pretend you're playing hide-n-seek, alright? Climb into the cabinet and don't come out until you hear a voice calling that you know, okay?"

It might seem weird that I wasn't scared of this strange man and that I listened to him, but I don't know what to say. It was easy to follow his commands and doing so just felt natural and smart.

The last thing I saw before closing the door, taking the space where the big mixing bowl usually sat, was the man turning around and going into the front room with such a zipping speed, I would have missed it should I have blinked.

The rest of the memory is even more hazy. Loud sounds, screams, angry yells, a snarl or two, more clattering and smashing, and then the loudest of all, a gunshot, filled the darkness around me.

I don't know how long I was in that cabinet, but I remember my legs tingled and ached. Carefully, I pushed around some dishes and found space to stretch my legs so they'd stop hurting, but then my butt hurt after that. Tears flowed down my face, and I shook so badly, I had to pick up a metal lid so it would stop clinking from my trembles.

At one point, the dark stranger came back. He peeked into the cabinet. The relief on his face as he saw me turned quickly into sadness. "Listen, doll. I'm so sorry. I've failed, but I promise I won't fail again. Stay here until your family comes for you. You'll be safe; I promise."

He left just as quickly as he'd appeared and I was alone, again.

I didn't know how long it was until my mom found me, and perhaps I'll never know since she won't talk about it, but I'm certain it was at least an hour later, which is a long time for a four-year-old. The door creaked open, letting in the warm kitchen light and my mom's worried face peered into the darkness I'd started to embrace.

"Oh, my baby girl!"

She pulled me out and we both sobbed into each other's hair as we hugged.

She wouldn't let me see what had happened in the front room that night, covering my head with her jacket as we walked out of the house.

I didn't even know my grandma was dead until I saw her ghost the next day. She looked the same, wearing the same clothes she'd had on that night, her hair styled in the same short, wavy curls, except she was blue, transparent, and her eyes pooled with such sadness unlike I'd ever seen before.

She only appeared for a few minutes that first time, sitting next to my mom on her bed as she sobbed into a pillow. Gran tried to comfort her and tell her she was okay and how much she loved us, but it was like Mom couldn't see or hear her.

I was playing on the floor with my dolls, but after Gran left, I crawled up next to my mom.

"Why didn't you talk to Gran? She was right here talking, and you didn't talk back."

My mom looked up and squinted. Her eyes were puffy and red. "What?"

"Gran was right here, and you didn't listen."

Looking back on this memory, I had to have scared my mom during a very emotional and tense time. I don't blame her for her reaction, but that doesn't mean the memory doesn't sting. The pain I felt from her response has echoed throughout the years, and I feel it every time I see another ghost, which since I'm cursed or whatever, happens to be a lot.

"Don't you dare say things like that! It's not funny!" She dropped the pillow and grabbed my shoulders so tightly her nails dug in through my thin t-shirt. "Dead people don't come back, and they don't talk! You get that out of your head, right now. We'll have no more nonsense talk of ghosts ever again!"

It occurs to me as I tell this story that I hadn't ever even said the word "ghost". In fact, at that point, I hadn't even realized that's what I was seeing. There was more to her anger than just me, but of course I didn't understand that at the time.

I learned several things that day that have managed to stick with me over the years. First, normal people don't talk about ghosts, at least not often and seriously. Second, normal people don't even see ghosts. Third, I am not normal.

My name is Hanna Sanchez, and I see dea—wait, is that copyright-ed? I can see ghosts.

Chapter 2

Eleven years later, it was my first day of 10th grade which meant I was going into high school. I was determined to be the most normal kid there. I probably would have succeeded if it hadn't been for meeting Brandon, but I'll get to him later.

I got up like most girls my age and ran around frantically getting myself together, worried I was going to be late. I shouldn't have worried about it and just accepted it as a fact. Trina was always late, and I didn't feel like getting to school without her as my buffer. She was a senior and had promised to help me find my way around.

"Trina! Open the door! I need to do my hair." I hammered on the bathroom door with my fist. I've heard tales of some girls who have their own bathrooms and don't have to share them with their sisters. I can't even imagine how awesome that would be.

As it was, I'd had to work around Trina's bathroom schedule my whole life. You think I'd be used to it and plan ahead, right?

"Just a second!" she yelled, the door and blow-dryer muffling her voice.

I fidgeted outside the door, having nothing else I could do to get ready. I'd put on my outfit that Trina had helped pick out—a black top with lace sleeves and a fitted pair of jeans. I'd even put my shoes on. At least I had taken a shower the night before. I'd gotten into that habit years ago knowing that I would never be able to take one in the morning unless I got up hours early.

A rush of humidity and the smell of fruity shampoo flew into the hall when she finally opened the door.

"Let me get my mascara on, and then I'll help you style your hair," Trina said, staring into the mirror like a fish with her mouth open, trying to get the mascara just right. She wore a brand-new top and parachute pants while the weird eye necklace she always wore dangled in between her collar bones as she leaned closer towards the mirror.

"We're going to be late." I might have whined.

"It's fine."

"Just worry about getting yourself ready. I can handle my hair." I put product in it to embrace the honey blonde waves while (hopefully) avoiding some of the frizz. I hadn't been as lucky to get beautifully smooth, chestnut hair like Trina and Mom had. I got my unruly, light hair from my dad, and while he kept it short to tame it, I didn't want to follow *that* trend.

Trina glanced at my efforts and gave me a look. "Whatever you say."

"I'd rather be on time than have perfectly curled hair."

"And that's where we're different. Being on time is overrated."

"Maybe having perfect hair is overrated."

We both laughed at my silliness.

Trina was still not finished by the time I'd fixed my hair, put on a little foundation, eyeliner, and grabbed my pink backpack, ready to head out the door.

"You look lovely," my mom said as she passed me in the kitchen where I was sitting at the table, waiting for Trina to finish.

Grandma's ghost shuffled quietly into the room, always following my mom around. The sadness in her eyes still filled me with guilt and shame, but I'd gotten used to ignoring her over the years.

"Thanks, Mom."

"Are you nervous for today?" She got out some bread and popped it into the toaster. "Want some toast?"

I ignored the second question in favor of the first. "A little. I feel like I'm invading Trina's territory. She's like the queen of the school and people probably expect me to be just like her."

Mom waved her hand dismissively as she looked for butter in the fridge. "Just be yourself. You keep trying to be like Trina, but she's her, and you are you."

I sighed and glanced down the hallway towards the bathroom. "That's the problem."

Dad scuffed his slippers as he came into the kitchen. "What's for breakfast?" He still wore his flannel pajamas, and his hair was smooshed on one side where he'd slept on it. He was a sociology professor and was able to pick his work hours, for the most part. He'd chosen not to have to go into work as early as most people did, wisely, I might add. He was not a morning person.

"There's bread for toast or you can have oatmeal if you want," Mom said while getting the coffee going.

"You should have gotten up early so he'd have a hot breakfast." Grandma's ghost shook her head.

I glanced at the clock and knew we should have left five minutes ago to be safely in my comfort zone. Thankfully, Trina bounded down the hallway with her purse and perfectly curled hair. It was shapely but not stiff, as if the perfect individual curls occurred naturally.

"Ready?" Trina's eyes sparkled with her grin, and it occurred to me she was probably super excited to start her last year of high school.

"Ready as I'll ever be." I sighed and stood up.

"Don't you want breakfast, girls?" Mom asked while stirring her coffee.

"No time. Love ya, Mom. Dad." Trina blew them kisses and flew out the door.

"Have a good day!" Mom called out after us.

"Stay away from boys!" Dad chimed in.

We both rolled our eyes where he couldn't see us.

The ride to school was rushed, and I wondered if we'd die before we ever made it. Thankfully, Trina managed to navigate her small Honda through the busy suburban streets, and we made it to the parking lot just as the first bell rang, signaling that we had five minutes before class would start.

"Ugh, Trina! I don't even know where my classes are. Why are we so late?" I slammed the door as I got out of the car.

"It's fine." Trina's long legs climbed out before the rest of her, and she glanced down at the schedule I had clutched in my hand.

"You have P.E. first. Yikes, that's the worst class to have first. Your look will be wilted for the rest of the day. Might as well just not try until class is over."

"Helpful."

"Just go to the gym. You won't be able to miss it. See you at lunch!" She waved as she turned towards her friends who had waited outside for her imminent arrival.

Not even the bright morning sunshine and fresh breeze could help me feel better as I made my way to the other end of the school where the building was taller and looked more like a gym, at least from the outside. Even if I could find the gym easily enough, what about the rest of my classes? Trina was supposed to help me figure out where all of them were. That was the whole point of having an older sibling who went to a school before you, right?

I was going to be that lame sophomore rushing around between classes trying to figure out where I was supposed to be going. If I got lost or was late to any of my classes, Trina was going to hear all about it. You think she'd be more invested in her little sister's reputation, and by extension, her own.

Guess not.

I found the gym easily enough and sat on the bleachers with the rest of the lost and younger looking students. They were spread out in ones and twos, and there was an awkward silence as we listened to a class on the other side of the gym with older students who were talking animatedly to each other. It was the obvious difference between a sophomore class of incoming students and a junior class who had already spent a year getting to know each other.

The sophomore class of Willow High School was constructed from two different junior high schools. They mushed us together into the same school which meant that I would see my friends from ninth grade, but that we'd also be around students we didn't know.

It appeared that my first class of the day didn't include anyone I knew. There was one kid I recognized, but I had no idea what his name was.

Luckily, I hadn't seen any ghosts yet. It didn't mean that the gym wasn't haunted, but that there weren't many out and about at that moment.

Thankfully, Coach Reed only lectured us that first day. Going through the rest of my classes post a two-mile run on the first day of school would have been the worst. Perhaps she was kind enough to understand that.

After class ended, and I'd had heard more than enough about why exercise was important, I left the gym, muttering to myself the information for my next class. I glanced at the schedule, and then put it back into my bag, refusing to be the kid who carried the schedule around with me all day, as if I didn't know where my classes were or something.

Which I didn't, of course, thanks to my oh-so-helpful sister.

My second period was history, and it was one of the classes I was actually looking forward to.

Searching over the heads of my bustling peers, I caught sight of the hallway labels. The school was laid out like a wheel with the cafeteria at the heart. The gym had been down one spoke of the wheel, and as I walked towards the center, I was intimidated by the chaotic activity. Students yelled and laughed and walked quickly down the halls. Of course, junior high had had a lot of activity between classes, but high school was on another level.

I dodged a group of older girls who were too immersed in their conversation to worry about trampling over a sophomore. Thick perfume followed in their wake, but I much preferred that scent after spending forty-five minutes in the gym.

"Hey, aren't you Trina's little sister?"

I found myself staring up at a tall senior, one of the boys that I'd seen hang with Trina and her friends. He was on the football team and had a dark tan on his already dark skin to prove it. His nearly black hair was cut short and styled neatly without too much product.

"Oh, hi. Yes, I am." I stepped towards the wall, out of the way of the flowing students. If you weren't careful, they'd trod right over you as if they were running from zombies. "I'm sorry. I don't know your name?"

He smiled, and the white of his teeth illuminated the whole hallway. It was so bright, I almost wished I had my sunglasses. I could see why Trina hung out with him. He was attractive and exuded an undercurrent of confidence and dare I say... sexuality? I hadn't explored much of that part of the human experience yet, but for some reason, this guy brought it straight to my mind.

"It's Caleb, and don't be sorry. I don't know yours either."

"It's, er—" I stuttered and blinked, too dazzled to have my wits, "Hanna!"

He laughed, but not in a mean way, just a teasing way. "Are you sure?"

"Yes, it's Hanna." I chuckled too, trying to recover.

"Alright, Hanna. Don't mind me noticing, but you look a little lost. Do you need some help?"

I would have felt relief at someone offering me help if it wasn't from some kind of Greek god, but I worked hard to focus and be gracious. "Oh, is it that obvious?"

He nodded with a smirk. "Pretty much all the sophomores do. It's all good."

"We probably seem really lame to you seniors." I fiddled with the strap of my bag, finally noticing other people around us again. Most of the girls were giving me side-eye, and it wasn't too hard to guess why.

"We've all been there, doll. Where you headed?"

"I have history next, room 140?"

"Ah, it so happens that I have class in the 40s, too, this period. I'll take you right there." He fell in step beside me but took the outside, putting me by the wall so he could buffer the stream of students. He was so tall everyone moved to avoid him, even the kids oblivious to anything but their phones.

"The 40s?"

"The school is like a big wheel and each hall is labeled by the numbers. Your history class is 140 which is down the 40s hall, just like 145 and 147. Does that make sense?"

I nodded, finally noticing that each spoke in the wheel had a number on the wall to indicate which group it was.

We headed towards the 40s, and I took mental notes of where the other numbers were so I could find my way around the rest of the day.

"Okay, I get it. Geez, it's really simple. I can't believe I missed that."

He laughed, the sound rumbling deep in his chest. "No worries."

We walked down the start of the 40s hall, and I began to worry about silence, but I didn't know what to say.

"Trina talks about you sometimes, but I'm a bit disappointed that she never told me how beautiful you are," Caleb said just as I was trying to come up with something to talk about.

His comment caught me off guard and blood rushed to my face. I could feel the heat in my skin and my eyes got wide. "Er—thank you. I'm nothing compared to Trina, though. All the boys think she's hot."

Caleb waved his hand in dismissal. "Hot and beautiful are two different things. Trina gets in her own way sometimes, but you're more content in your own skin. I like your vibes. Anyway, here's 140. Think you'll be able to find your next class?"

I shrugged, trying to play it cool, but my blushing face and awkward stance were sure to give me away. "Sure. Now that you've pointed out the system, I think I can do it. Thanks for your help!"

I dashed into the classroom, eager to get away from the pressure of his coolness. His chuckle chased behind me, and I was smiling as I slid into a chair near the back.

My heart was racing, and I focused on breathing and stilling my trembling fingers. I struggled for a second to open my bag for a pen and paper, but I finally got it. It helped me calm down more by focusing on being grateful that I hadn't been late. I would have been blushing then for an entirely different reason.

I looked around the room and noticed a few familiar faces. The most familiar was Noah Jenkins. He hung out with my group of friends and was probably the most popular kid there. I know how cliché it sounds, having a crush on the most popular kid. I didn't mean to. I just couldn't help it. It was his fault for having such a strong jawline, perfect brown hair that fell into his hazel eyes at all the right moments, and a smile that drew me in like a mosquito to a bug zapper.

Okay, so I might have been a little boy crazy. What can I say? I couldn't help it.

Noah gave me a smile and a small wave when he noticed I was staring at him. I'm sure the smile I gave back was a bit lopsided, but I did my best.

"Welcome to World History. I'm Mr. Tyler, and I'll be your teacher," a man said from the front of the class.

Mr. Tyler was short and wiry. He was balding on top and kept the rest of his hair shorn short so you could tell there was just a bit of fuzz there. He wore glasses that he liked to wave around when he was gesturing about a particularly poignant point.

The students quieted and straightened to look at him. I expected him to launch into a lecture about why history was so important and why we should buy into what he was trying to teach us, but instead, he took a refreshing route.

"Someone explain to me why interviews are a helpful aspect of history. And I don't expect you to raise your hands. We'll be having adult discussions here like normal conversations." Mr. Tyler appraised our class over the top of his spectacles.

"They get information and the story straight from the source." I surprised myself by speaking first, but the question had caught my interest.

"Exactly, Miss?" His bushy eyebrows raised in question.

"Miss Sanchez."

"Miss Sanchez, great. It might take me a while, but I'll learn the names. Someone else tell me why getting information straight from the source is important."

"So we can know the facts first-hand, instead of just through word of mouth," Bree North, a girl from my middle school that I didn't know too well, spoke from a few desks away from me. "Otherwise, things can get distorted and changed around."

Mr. Tyler nodded. "And you are?"

"Bree North," she said with an official nod.

"Excellent. How much of history do you think has been distorted?"

"Isn't there a saying that 'the winners write history'?" Noah asked.

My body warmed as I heard his voice, and I allowed myself a small glimpse in his direction since he was talking. It was a lot less obvious if you were gazing upon someone's good looks if they were already talking to the class. It wasn't creepy at all, right?

"Ah, quite so. What does *that* mean?" Mr. Tyler bounced on his toes to emphasize the word "that".

"It means that sometimes the—" Just as I began to answer the question, the small hairs on the back of my neck prickled. A loud voice interrupted the classroom discussion. Once I caught sight of the speaker, however, I realized only I could hear him, thanks to my not-so-cool superpowers.

"And so, students, you must remember to always be vigilant. Never let your guard down, or you could end up like Abraham Lincoln." The ghostly newcomer paced in front of the class, hands behind his back and shoulders straight. His lecturing voice bellowed loudly. He was oblivious to Mr. Tyler as he walked through him and back, addressing students that had long since grown up. The ghost teacher wore a tweed suit in a style I didn't recognize but could only assume was of an earlier generation, perhaps in the early days of the school's existence.

"Yes, Miss Sanchez?" Mr. Tyler prompted me to continue with another raise of his eyebrows, an expression I was learning he did often.

Heat rushed to my face, and I felt a trickle of sweat bead down my back. Everyone was looking at me, waiting for me to finish my sentence—everyone, which also happened to include Noah. Someone giggled behind me, and I swallowed.

"I'm sorry. Yes, it means that sometimes history isn't correct since the winners are the survivors and the ones able to tell the stories." I stopped short of saying more because it was difficult for me to focus on Mr. Tyler and what I was saying while the ghost was loudly explaining what happened to the nation after Lincoln's assassination.

"The country was reeling. How could this happen to the most important man in the world?" the ghost bellowed.

Mr. Tyler continued, heedless of the other teacher in the room. "Right. The survivors can tell the story of how they saw it, and how they proved themselves to be the good guys in the end. Can you imagine what stories the Nazis would tell if they had won World War II? What would history look like from their perspective?"

The class erupted as several students joined the discussion. I tried to focus on what they were saying and probably caught most of it, but it was difficult because of the loudness of the other teacher. I was quite impressed with his ability to bellow so long without losing his voice.

Later, I chewed on my lip as I walked to my next class, third period English. It was in room 170, but I was easily able to find the 70s after Caleb's previous instructions. I was lost in thought, heedless to the other students who sometimes bumped into me.

It was unusual for a ghost to stick around for so long. Usually, ghosts only flitted in and out, sometimes even disappearing mid-sentence. This ghost had stayed for at least ten minutes and then had come back during the last half of class. I was worried about what it all meant, and if I was going to have trouble paying attention in Mr. Tyler's class. I didn't want to have another embarrassing moment like that in front of Noah.

As I turned down the 70s hall, I shook my head, silently chiding myself for getting so distracted by a ghost. I had battled ghosts all my life. It should have been easy to tune him out, no matter how loud his lecture was.

"Are you arguing with yourself again in public?" Trina said as she lightly bumped into my shoulder, appearing from nowhere. "I told you what that does for your image."

"Aren't you worried about how your little sister is doing on her first day of school when her older sister didn't even help her find her classes?" I gave her a look as we walked down the hallway.

"Oh, you figured it out just fine. I can't be there to hold your hand all the time, now can I? I might be a bit of a flake, but at least I don't look like I'm gazing into outer space all the time."

"Well, at least my friends don't look like they came straight out of a magazine all the time. Are your friends even real or just perfect robots?"

Trina burst into a throaty chuckle. "Was that supposed to be an insult?"

I huffed and turned away from her, heading towards my classroom. Her laughter followed me down the hall as I passed her friends that were going to meet her. Heat flushed my cheeks as I thought about Trina telling them what I had said. I glanced up to reassure myself Caleb wasn't among them and was relieved to see he wasn't. I really hoped she didn't tell him what I'd said.

It sucked being the younger sister sometimes. We'd see who got the last laugh, though, when she got wrinkles and age spots first.

Chapter 3

Thankfully my English and art classes passed smoothly without ghosts or other cute guys. I blessed Caleb's name to whatever god was listening as I found each class easily. There were several students I recognized in class, but I didn't see any of my friends.

I was beginning to wonder if all my friends, except Noah, had somehow gone to another high school. I wished I had asked to see their schedules over summer to see if we had any classes together, but the thought hadn't occurred to me.

Perhaps I did spend too much time thinking about invisible people.

Lunch finally arrived and there was no question about where *that* was being held.

I stopped by the bathroom on my way to the cafeteria and checked over my appearance, making sure nothing was out of line. My hair still wasn't falling down my shoulders like a beautiful, sleek, cascading waterfall—more like a bumpy road with a few weeds growing in the median. It was the best I could do with what I had. Mostly, I was just checking for boogers or anything out of the ordinary.

It was important to attend lunch looking as good as I could, but there was another reason I took some time in the bathroom, despite the several ghosts that haunted it. A girl's high school bathroom was probably one of the saddest places to be stuck for eternity as your haunt, but there sure were a lot of them that must have been trying to relive their high school days.

The other reason was one I would never share with my family or friends, no matter how close we got. I waited out the first few minutes of lunch while everyone got in line and grabbed food. My stomach growled as the smell wafted down the hall, but I refused to acknowledge it.

Food was the enemy. Food made people fat, and judging by the genetics in my family, it wouldn't take much for me to get there.

When I finally made it to the cafeteria, it didn't take long to survey the room and find where my friends were sitting. They had claimed a table off to the side, away from the bustling line waiting to get food.

"Hey, guys." I plopped down my bag and slid into a spot on the end of the bench.

"Nice of you to join us. What, did you get lost?" Andrea said as her perfectly colored blonde hair shone in the overhead lights.

I resisted the urge to wince as her words were probably truer than she realized. Obviously, the cafeteria was easy enough to find, but yeah, I had gotten lost that day. Andrea was the last person I was going to tell, though.

Everyone at the table turned their eyes to me at Andrea's direction. Their gazes felt heavy, but none so heavy as that of Noah's. He was sitting across from Andrea, half a sandwich still in his hand. His perfect hair hung in front of his eyes like I loved, and he flashed me a friendly smile.

"Nah, just had to stop by and make out with a senior. You know how they can't resist us little sophomores." I tried to sound confident and fun, but I'm not sure how well I pulled it off. Twisting the cap of my water bottle open, I tried to appear unaffected by everyone's attention, even though my fingers trembled slightly.

Andrea glared at me. "Funny."

Yup, it hadn't come out like I'd wanted. Instead, I'd just insulted her somehow, but I wasn't sure what went wrong or how to fix it.

"Actually, I did see her with Caleb Jackson earlier. Maybe she *was* making out with a senior." Randi raised her eyebrows scandalously.

Everyone looked at me again like they were studying an ant under a microscope. I hoped I didn't get burned by the sunlight.

I laughed it off and waved my hand in the air. "Oh, no. He's a friend of my sister's. He was just saying 'hi'."

Andrea, Randi, and Stephanie's expressions told me they weren't sure what to believe while Noah's eyes narrowed slightly. Whatever that meant.

"Anyway, how was everyone's first bit of school? Any teachers we're going to hate this year?" I tried to steer the conversation away from myself and took another nonchalant swig of my water bottle.

"Did you guys see Carly's hair?" Andrea turned to the others, and while she completely ignored my questions, I was just grateful they weren't all focused on me anymore.

It was hard to be sure sometimes what Andrea or the others were thinking. It was important to say just the right things or else you might get teased later. Sometimes you got teased right then. Being laughed at felt a lot different than being laughed with, let me tell you. I seemed to mess up a lot around them, probably because I was trying too hard to get Noah to like me.

But a girl's gotta try, right?

For the rest of lunch, I enjoyed conversation with my friends and studiously ignored the cafeteria ghost who was peering over the shoulders of the lunch ladies, making sure they were doing their jobs right.

There were three more classes before school was finally out for the day. Fifth was chemistry which looked like it was going to be a drag. Randi turned out to be in my sixth period French class. We sat together but didn't have much time for talking since the teacher launched right into French on our first day, and we were furiously trying to figure out what in the world she was saying.

I bumped into Andrea on my way to geometry and was happy to see we were headed to the same place.

"Hey, I just saw Randi in French. I'm glad to see we have a class together, too." I gave Andrea a friendly smile, but I hoped it wasn't too eager. I didn't want her to think I was a clingy friend.

"I'm glad to see you, too." She combed her fingers through her blonde hair as we waited in our seats for class to start. It looked smooth and soft even after a whole day of schooling. She probably took as long as Trina to get ready in the mornings, if that were even possible. Andrea also had judging green eyes and a bone structure that could make any model jealous. I could certainly see why the other kids in my class followed her, including me.

"You know how terrible I am at math." She gave me a knowing look with a side smile.

The thing is I totally did know how terrible she was at math. She could probably do better if she'd apply herself, but in our class last year, she spent most of the time texting underneath the desk and then copied my homework later. I didn't mind, though. It gave her more reason to need me around. Sometimes, the need even felt a little good—at least I knew I was good for something other than talking to ghosts no one else could see.

Our math teacher, Mr. Mink, was the typical middle-aged man that had obviously been a nerd during his school years. His glasses were always a little crooked and he spoke in a nasally tone.

The last class went painfully slow. The classroom was too warm, and I felt the day's exhaustion sink into me. It was difficult to stay awake.

Finally, Mr. Mink assigned us a worksheet to review what we should have learned last year and dismissed class.

"Hey, have you been to the skatepark down the road?" Andrea asked me as we packed up our stuff.

"Nope, never been there. Driven by it lots of times, of course, but never stopped."

"Perfect. Everyone goes there now. Let's meet there in a few minutes. We'll go through the math homework together."

If I thought the halls were chaotic before, it was nothing compared to the rush of the end of school. I spent several minutes trying to figure out the locker system and finally found the one I'd been assigned. I couldn't keep carrying all the heavy books I'd gotten throughout the day, and I didn't need to take any of them home for homework except the one for English.

It took me a few tries, but I finally figured how to open the locker from the vague instructions on the assignment sheet.

I sighed with relief when I could put all the books down and wondered why I hadn't taken time to do it earlier.

Sometimes I wasn't the smartest crayon in the box.

After that, I walked straight to the skatepark. It was only two blocks away from school, but I had never spent time there. I was more of a mall person, or even better, I enjoyed a quiet library. The skatepark was outside, and living in Virginia, that usually meant humidity and mosquitoes. It was early fall, but still plenty warm enough to collect sweat and a few itchy bites.

Andrea wasn't there when I arrived, but there were several kids skating or walking around. I wasn't sure what to do when I stepped through the gate, and I felt self-conscious, hoping no one was noticing the random, lonely girl looking around. Thankfully, there were picnic tables on the other side of the skating area. I made my way to the tables, through the surrounding grass, trying to look like I belonged there.

It was hard to look cool while walking and watching the skaters zip and zoom all over the cement at the same time. There were several curves and hills and walls that the skaters handled like the laws of physics didn't exist. Of course, a few fell here and there, saved by their knee pads or helmets, but most of them cruised and flipped with amazing speed.

I almost tripped once because there was a dip in the grass, and my eyes were following a particularly skilled skater. He flew up the wall closest to me, went airborne, flipped his skateboard around, and landed in time to catch the board and skate back down the slope.

I felt blood rush to my face after my almost trip and decided to keep my eyes focused on the ground while I was walking, instead of on the skaters.

Picking the table in the back, near the fence, I plopped my bag down and sat on the top, my feet resting on the bench. I pulled out the math homework, a pencil, and a notebook to write on while it rested on my knees.

It was difficult to concentrate on the assignment for several reasons. One, I kept looking up for Andrea, waiting for her to arrive so I didn't feel too uncomfortable sitting by myself. Two, the skaters were impressive and loud. Three, there was a ghost.

He was a 90s skater boy. His body blinked in and out and it was hard to follow his path at first. He popped up in the air, twisted around, landed back on the cement, and disappeared again. Then I saw him zip through the bottom, easily passing through the curves, clearing a hill, and landing cleanly, only to disappear again.

The ghost was out of place compared to the other skaters. While they wore modern athletic gear and basketball shorts, this kid was wearing gigantic jean pants. The legs flared out and the tips of his worn skater shoes poked out of the bottoms. He wore a band t-shirt that I'd never heard of over a long-sleeved shirt. His light hair was spiked all over his head. A wallet chain hooked on the front of his pants, trailed down the side and went into his pocket, moving and swaying with his motion.

The more I watched him, the less he disappeared. He was transparent and glowing vaguely blue as all the ghosts did, but he was becoming more stable. Soon, I could map out his path and knew where he would appear next if he faded for a moment. Eventually, he didn't disappear at all.

I glanced between him and the math, trying to focus on one problem at a time. Luckily, I wasn't too rusty and could remember how to do most of the homework.

At first, he kept the same path and pattern in his skating routine, perhaps stuck in the habitual route he took while he was alive, but at one point, he made a deviation. When he neared the curve that happened to be closest to the tables, something went wrong, and his skateboard flew out of his hands, disappeared into the air, and the guy went tumbling over the cement.

I winced at his wipe-out and must have had an empathic expression on my face for a moment too long. His eyes locked on mine as he righted himself, and I felt his focus zoom in.

Immediately, I darted my gaze away and pretended I had been watching someone else, someone alive, who had tripped up.

The ghost kid wasn't fooled, though, and as he stood up, wiping the invisible dust off his behind, his eyes never left my face.

Chapter 4

I was saved by Noah and Andrea walking towards me. I was relieved to see them but also annoyed that they had come together.

They hadn't officially labeled themselves as a couple yet, but everyone noticed how they spent so much time together. It was probably only a matter of time before they changed their relationship status.

I usually pretended not to notice, hoping that my inattention would somehow make the situation change. I guess I did that with a lot of things these days.

"Hey, guys," I greeted too loudly, hoping to deter the ghost from bothering me.

It didn't. Curious, he followed behind my friends.

"Hi, Hanna." Noah gave me a friendly smile that I tried hard not to read into too much.

Andrea glanced at Noah's reaction and gave me a quick, fake smile. "We usually sit at this table."

They stopped at a spot to the left, two rows up from the table I had picked. I couldn't see any reason why that one was better than mine, but it was fine.

"Cool." I grabbed my bag and joined them at the appointed table.

Andrea sat next to Noah, their backs leaning on the table as they looked out at the skatepark. She made sure she was so close that their forearms and knees were touching. I was wise enough to sit on Andrea's other side instead of next to Noah. I didn't want to give her any more reason to suspect I liked him.

The ghost kid tilted his head in thought as he sat down at the table in front of ours. Instead of facing the skaters like we were, he was facing me. If I were to look at the skatepark, I'd have to look directly through him.

I tried very hard to keep my gaze from focusing on him.

"Have you finished the assignment?" Andrea glanced over at my paper as she opened the notebook she'd been carrying and sorted through the folder.

Grateful for the distraction, I handed her my paper. "I've got most of them. I'm not sure about number seven, but we can double-check it together."

"Mmhmm." Andrea took the homework from me and started scribbling my answers onto her paper.

I pretended not to notice. "Are the others coming? You said everyone hangs out here now?"

Andrea shrugged, her loose shirt slipped down over one shoulder, showing a slim bra strap. Noah's eyes flicked towards it and then back down to his phone.

Unsure what to do with her answer, I let my eyes roam over the skatepark again, careful to slide past the ghost who was still staring right at us. The skaters flew around the cement like pendulums on a clock and were nearly as well-timed.

Andrea's scribbles became louder as silence edged into our conversation. I shifted on the bench. "So, when's football practice starting, Noah?"

He glanced up from his phone for a second to give me a nod. "We've been working through the summer. I actually have to meet the boys in half an hour or so."

Andrea's hand slowed after my question, as if her brain was making room for thoughts other than just how to write numbers.

"That doesn't give you much time to hang out." I tried to sound uninterested and that I was merely using conversation to avoid the awkwardness of the situation, instead of hanging on to his every word.

Noah shrugged. "We need to train or else we won't get any better."

Andrea passed my paper back and closed her notebook. She leaned out further on the bench, just enough that she blocked my view of Noah. "Your answers all look good to me."

"I'll bet they did," the ghost said, his hand resting on his chin as he rolled his eyes.

I tightened my lips in a firm line to keep from reacting to his words. "Thank you. I tried my best, at least."

I put the paper back into my bag, careful not to crumple it, and pulled the zipper tight.

"I can feel your power, you know." The ghost tapped his fingers on the table, not making any sound. "I haven't been this stable in years."

I kept ignoring him. "Did you guys bring a skateboard? It seems kind of weird to sit here at a skatepark without a skateboard."

"Do I look like I skate?" Andrea put a territorial hand on Noah's knee. "Besides, we don't have time to fool around. Like he said, we've got practice."

"Oh." I nodded. "So why are we here?"

The ghost sighed. "Obviously to get your homework answers. Look at them. Do you think they're really here to hang with the cool kids?"

Andrea stood and adjusted the books in her arm. "Seemed like a cool place. Maybe one day Noah can bring his board and show me some cool tricks."

"Oh, I'm sure he has all kinds of 'cool' tricks to show you." The ghost wiggled his eyebrows up and down suggestively.

I cleared my throat to force the laughter away and stood as well. It felt weird having her tower over me while I was still sitting. "Right. Makes sense."

"No, it doesn't," Ghost Boy said.

Andrea grabbed Noah's hand, which was still clutching his phone as he scrolled. He let her pull him to stand.

"Guess we'll see you at lunch tomorrow." Andrea flashed me a socially obligated smile.

"I'll walk out with you guys." I grabbed my bag and followed them through the maze of tables.

The ghost stood as we passed him and fell in line behind me. "Are these goons really your friends?"

Andrea kept her fingers laced through Noah's while giving me an annoyed look. Noah also glanced at me, but his expression was more apologetic than taunting.

The skaters didn't even distract us as we walked towards the gate and back to the street.

"Thanks for the homework help." Noah pulled his hand from Andrea's as we reached the sidewalk and gave me a wave.

"I mean, I didn't help you, but sure, no problem." His kindness overshadowed Andrea's rudeness, and I smiled genuinely, glad at least someone had manners.

Andrea shot me another fake smile. "See you later."

Noah waved as she dragged him back towards the school.

"Have fun trying to breathe with her leash around your neck," Ghost Boy hollered as he waved at my retreating friends like a grandma waving to her grandchildren.

I couldn't help a smirk from escaping my lips.

"Aha! I knew you could hear me!"

I glanced around, careful to search the street for any other ghosts. I didn't want a mob descending upon me because I couldn't hold in a laugh. "Fine. Good for you. Yes, I can hear you."

"Wow, it's so crazy! How can you hear me? You can see me, too, right?" Ghost Boy danced in a circle around me like a ridiculous chicken. "I knew you could see me the second I wiped out on my board. Then you were like all pretending not to see me, but it was too late. I just knew it."

I sighed but couldn't help smiling—his happiness was so carefree and contagious. "Do you want a trophy or something?"

"My name is Brandon. I've—"

And just like that, he fizzled out. Ghosts didn't usually last too long, and Ghost Boy had been solid for longer than any other ghost I'd seen so far, except for Grandma. I wasn't surprised to see him wink out of existence, but I had to admit, I was a little disappointed.

The whole walk home I chided myself for wanting to talk to a ghost. What was wrong with me? I knew better. Talking to ghosts only led to chaos and overwhelming emotions as other ghosts zeroed in on me.

Plus, there was the added danger of appearing insane to everyone else who was actually alive. There were just no upsides to talking to ghosts.

I decided it was a good thing that we weren't going to hang out at the skatepark often. I should avoid Brandon as much as possible.

Chapter 5

Dinner with my family was always the hardest part of my day. I know that it shouldn't have been that way, and it wasn't all my family's fault, but that's how it felt, nevertheless.

It's not like my family is horrible. I'm aware enough to know that there are much worse family situations out there than mine. But there's a special power families have to get on each other's nerves.

If you have a sister, you might know what I mean. Sisters seem to be the best at knowing just what to say to get you angry.

"Hanna, don't you think Mom's casserole is delicious?" Trina peered over at my plate while we sat at the table.

I glanced at mom who was grabbing a water pitcher from the fridge. "Yes, it's delicious. Mom really is the best cook ever. Except for maybe Grandma, of course."

Right after I said it, I regretted those last words when Grandma's ghost perked up and focused her attention on our conversation, instead of just dejectedly following my mom around like she usually did. Grandma's ghost had followed Mom since that terrible night. Most of the ghosts I encountered were usually stuck in one place, a haunt as I called it, but Grandma's ghost was the first and only ghost, that I so far had seen, haunting a person.

I'll admit that I didn't have a lot of experience with ghosts and their haunts, but as far as I could tell, some rule of the ghost universe said they had to be tied to a place. I could only guess as to how my grandma was tied to a person.

I'll also admit that I had a deep-seeded guilt for ignoring my grandma these many years. She always looked so lost, her shoulders hunched, her hands clasped together tightly, and her eyes vigilantly watching my mom's life.

My mom and grandma shared the same chestnut hair color, but past that, they were very different. My grandma had been a timid lady, conforming to the pressures of conservative society to be a "proper" housewife, putting her husband and children's needs high above her own (although there are some family rumors of an odd hobby she'd had). My mom was quite the opposite. She was fiery, stubborn, and did what made her happy, uncaring of gossip from family or neighbors.

"Then why aren't you eating?" Trina raised a slim, perfectly shaped eyebrow at me.

I gave her a look, hoping she'd get the message to mind her own business.

Mom came back to the table and put down the pitcher. She spared me a glance but looked at my dad. "How is that article coming along?"

Grandma peered around Mom's shoulder. "Surely he's had a rough day at work. Look at the bags under his eyes. When grandpa got like that, I'd always have a foot bath ready."

Dad kept his eyes on his phone while shoveling a bite of casserole and beans into his mouth. "Good," he said around the food.

I should have felt relief that Mom hadn't caught Trina's hints, but I didn't. Mom's tone told me she had negative feelings of some kind. Dinners had been tense lately, and it was the only place where Mom and Dad were together during the day where Trina and I had a full view of their interactions.

Mom continued to stare at my dad, as if waiting for him to say more. He kept scrolling and eating, clueless.

She huffed and sat down, finally serving herself the food she'd spent an hour making after she'd come home from work.

"Caleb said he ran into you at school today." Trina broke the silence and looked at me with a knowing smile.

"Oh, did he mention that? What did he say?"

Trina laughed and shook her head. "You're just like the rest of them. Caleb shoots a girl a smile and that's it, they're in love."

"Am not!" I glanced at my mom, surprised she hadn't jumped into our conversation for more details. Normally she loves hearing about our lives, but she was staring into her beans so viciously I was afraid they'd catch on fire. "Besides, if my sister had done her sisterly duty and showed me the layout of the school, I wouldn't have needed his help. In a way, it's your fault."

"Eh, you figured it out. No biggie." She shrugged and then glanced at Dad. "I thought we had a no phones rule at the table. If Dad has his, I should get to have mine."

"It's for work," Dad said mechanically around another bite of food. "I'm trying to find information on a local family for my next article."

"Didn't you have time to do that at the office today?" Mom's tone was icy.

He sighed, finally putting down the phone. "I don't know what you want from me, Michelle. You're always checking in about my research, but then you get upset with me when I work on it. You know my office time is filled with student appointments or grading papers. There's only so much time in the day. How do you expect me to get all of this done?"

Mom's eyes sparked, and I knew that look from personal experience. "Perhaps if you spent less time watching TV or playing phone games, you might actually be able to get something done."

Grandma stood behind Mom and began wringing her hands again at the fire in my mom's voice. "Just let it go. He's the man of the house."

"Have you ever written a professional article? Do you even understand how long it takes to grade hundreds of students' papers? I'm sure taking pictures all day is just *so* exhausting."

I winced and knew this was a fight I didn't want to see. "I've got lots of homework to do. Thanks for the food, Mom. It was delicious."

I hopped up, tossed my uneaten food into the trash, put the plate into the sink, and dashed away to my bedroom while my mom rained down words of fire and brimstone at my dad.

"Wow, I'm so sorry, Mr. High and Mighty, I had no idea how difficult work was for you. Perhaps you've just gone into the wrong field—"

I shut my door and popped in earbuds to drown out their fight. It wasn't a new topic in the house, but it didn't usually get so heated. Music poured into my brain, and I turned it as loud as it needed to be so I couldn't hear my mom and dad yelling at each other.

My stomach grumbled from only drinking water all day, but I stood in the mirror and told my stomach to grow some eyes. It was clear that I didn't need food. I could pinch the skin on my stomach, and my thighs wobbled if I shook my legs.

I was certain Andrea's body was perfect. Noah was obviously attracted to her and if I were going to compete at all, I needed to be perfect. There wasn't much I could do with my face, and I didn't make enough allowance money to buy a new wardrobe or fix my unruly wavy hair. I could, however, make sure I was fit and thin.

Staring at myself in the mirror helped quiet the hunger in my stomach, and I flopped onto my bed to do homework. I riffled through my backpack until I found my English book, *1984*, and tried to focus on reading the words.

My brain had other ideas as it kept drifting through different images that I'd seen during the day. The first was the ghost from history class. The ghost had grown stronger the longer I was there, just like Brandon had when I'd been watching him. The teacher was loud and abrasive, and I didn't know how I was going to be able to concentrate on Mr. Tyler's words and the discussions going on around me while the rigid, ancient teacher was prattling on.

What was I going to do about it? Could I do anything about it? Was I doomed to fail one of my favorite classes?

It didn't help that Noah had been there to witness my distraction this morning. I couldn't begin to imagine what he thought of me.

Frustrated with the whole situation, I turned to the one place that had more answers than I would know what to do with. Surely, I could find a solution on the internet.

I typed in "how to get rid of a ghost" and sure enough, there were more results than I could read. I should have been doing my English homework, but this was way more interesting.

Some of the pages made me laugh in their absurdity. Other pages made me think, while even more made the hairs on my neck stand up. I had to look around my room just to make sure a ghost hadn't appeared while I was reading.

Thankfully, my room was the one place I hadn't seen any ghosts. It was my sanctuary, and I really hoped I never lived in a haunted place in the future. I really needed space I could be myself in.

As I read several articles, the research became less interesting, and more anxiety inducing. I compiled a list of ideas from the articles and a possible set of steps emerged that made me frown.

The first step was easy enough, and I was determined to do that one thoroughly in hopes I wouldn't need to progress to the other steps. I needed some sage, but not just any sage would do. Some pages didn't specify, but I read enough to determine that I needed white sage, organically sourced.

I looked up places I could find organic white sage and made a tentative plan. The store was closed this late in the day, so I would have to go after school the next day. Hopefully I could ignore the loud ghost well enough tomorrow during history, otherwise Noah, and the rest of my class, would know I was crazy.

Chapter 6

The next day was Tuesday, and it started with the same routine. Before I left for school, I gave myself a stern talking-to in the mirror.

I stared at my eyes which I had affectionately deemed the color of "mud puddle while the sun reflects off the surface". My mom had baulked at the description when I'd told her, but she hadn't realized I didn't mean it as a bad thing. It was just what they looked like.

"Now, listen here. You're in the prime of life. The choices you make now could determine the rest of your life. You're cute, getting thin, smart, and friendly. People want to be your friend and you are worthy of having good friends. You are alive and human and therefore, should be talking and listening to other live humans. Those ghosts will go away if you ignore them. They don't exist outside your mind. They aren't there. Focus on the real people around you and you'll be fine."

I nodded, agreeing with myself and spun away from the mirror, grabbed my bag and headed to school.

I didn't bother to wait for Trina who was still in the bathroom. The night before I'd gathered all my bathroom supplies I would need to get ready and put them in my bedroom so I wouldn't have to wait for her to finish her beautifying process.

I suppose I was finally learning.

While it took no time to drive to school, I didn't have a car, so I walked the seven or so blocks it took to get there. Even doing that was better than waiting for Trina and being late. The cool morning was pleasant, and I had left early enough that the walk didn't bother me. It was refreshing to have the peaceful quiet to myself as the sun spilled through the leaves and dazzled the sidewalks.

I felt a tad more comfortable inside the chaotic halls than I had the day before, but it was still overwhelming. I stopped by my locker to get the books I'd need for the next few classes, worried about having time to be at my locker between every class because some of them were on the other end of the building. Perhaps I'd level up to doing that when I was completely comfortable with my routine, but for now, I just grabbed what I needed for the first few classes and headed to the gym.

We changed in the locker room into our gym clothes. There was some friendly chatter between the girls and my ears perked up when one of them mentioned my friends.

"Well, we all know that Noah and Andrea will go to homecoming together. They're always together," one girl with pink pigtails said as she pulled up her socks.

"They do hang out a lot, but they could just be friends?" The other girl had her hair in a low ponytail and was tying up her tennis shoes.

"They're just friends." I stood from tying my own shoes. "I hang out with both of them, and they're just friends."

Pigtails raised her eyebrow at me, but I wasn't sure if it was because I butted into their conversation or if she didn't believe me.

Ponytail had the decency to look uncomfortable after having been caught talking about my friends.

"Oh, right. I think I've seen you with them." Pigtails studied me briefly. "Are you on the cheer squad with Andrea or something?"

"Unfortunately, I have the coordination of a newborn giraffe, and cheerleading is not in my future, but Andrea and Randi are nice enough to hang out with me anyway."

I found myself walking with Pigtails and Ponytail out of the locker room and into the gym. They laughed at my joke, and I hoped I'd found some girls to at least chat with during P.E., so it wasn't that awkward silence I'd grown to love so much.

We ran around the gym for a while, and I stayed with Pigtails and Ponytail, whose names turned out to be Emma and Addison. Addy was the one with the pink pigtails and after getting to know them, they seemed all right, even if they had been talking about my friends behind their backs.

My second day in the gym yielded a few ghosts but thankfully they weren't troublesome. A coach blinked in and out, and one time he blew his whistle so loud I stopped running and looked around for what was happening.

Emma bumped into me, and we laughed it off.

"Like I said, a clumsy giraffe."

As P.E. neared its end, I grew anxious for history class. I really hated having gym before the only class I had with Noah, but I tried not to run too fast and get too sweaty. Trina had been right about having P.E. for the first period of the day.

It really sucked.

I used a towel to dry myself off as much as I could, lathered on deodorant, and spritzed a few squirts of perfume in hopes I could recover from the stink of exercise.

As I walked through the halls, I took several deep breaths. I wasn't sure which I was more nervous about— getting to see Noah or getting distracted by the loud ghost again. Either way, I was nervous.

Caleb bumped lightly into my shoulder. "Hey, you."

"Oh, hey, Caleb." I smiled, hoping I looked normal and not hyperventilating from my run and nerves.

"You don't look as lost as yesterday. Did you find the rest of your classes all right?" He looked at me kindly, and I noticed his eyes were a pleasant brown, warm enough to get lost in.

"Yes, no thanks to my sister and much thanks to you."

He chuckled. "I'm glad"

"You don't seem like Trina's usual friends."

"What's that supposed to mean?" He said it with a teasing smile, so I knew he wasn't upset.

"I'm sure you know. She doesn't usually pick very friendly people to hang out with. I can't remember the last time one of her friends even talked to me, and they were at our house almost all summer. One even drank the last of the milk and burped instead of apologizing when I didn't have any for my cereal."

"Sounds about right."

We laughed, and I was wearing another smile as I walked into history class. Caleb had helped distract the nerves for a bit, but they came right back as I walked into the room.

The ghost teacher was standing with a straight back, arms folded behind him in a military stance, and his eyes were scrutinizing everyone who walked into the classroom. I couldn't be sure if he were looking at his old students in his mind, or if it was the current students he could see.

Either way, I made sure to slide my eyes straight across him and not engage in any eye contact.

"Sit down. Backs straight. Ladies, make sure to keep those dresses unwrinkled," the ghost barked, and I felt bad for his students from the past. He must have been a difficult teacher, or maybe they all were back in the day.

"Good morning, ladies and gents." Mr. Tyler walked from his desk to the front of the room. "Take a seat. Take a seat."

Noah waved me over from his spot in the back and while unspoken social protocol suggested that I should take the same seat that I'd had the day before, that lesser rule was discarded in favor of the-not-snubbing-my-friend-and-boy-I-liked rule.

I probably looked like a dork with a big grin on my face as I slid into the seat next to him. He smiled, too, but it was much more normal, I'm sure.

"Who were you just talking to?" Noah peered out into the hallway.

"Oh, that was Caleb. He's a friend of my sister's. Why? Are you jealous?" I teased him, but immediately felt stupid for saying that. Of course he wasn't jealous. He was crushing on Andrea, right?

Noah gave a polite chuckle but was saved from having to answer by class starting.

"Who did the reading last night?" Mr. Tyler half-sat on the desk in the front of the classroom. His hip and one leg rested on the top while the other leg still stayed on the ground.

"Let's begin where we left off yesterday," the ghost teacher also began class, and I took a deep breath, trying to focus myself on the teacher that mattered. "Andrew Johnson was now president. Union soldiers were hunting for John Wilkes Booth. They were headed to Southern Maryland and—"

The ghost kept going on about Booth and his voice was so much louder than Mr. Tyler's or any student who was answering his questions. I found myself squinting my eyes in order to hear better. I know that doesn't make sense, but sometimes I do it when I really wanted to focus on something. I'm not the only one, right?

"Hey, you okay?" Noah nudged the top of my foot with his, careful to keep his voice down.

"Huh?" I probably looked at him like he had six eyes and three noses.

"Uh, just you look a little... uncomfortable?"

"Finally, they set fire to the barn. Herold surrendered, but Booth, the coward, stayed inside," the ghost lectured.

"What's going on back there?" Mr. Tyler had noticed we were talking, and I couldn't take all the chaos.

I stood and grabbed my bag. "I'm sorry, Mr. Tyler. I'm getting a migraine, and I really need to go to the nurse's office before I throw up all over my desk."

I must have looked flushed enough to be convincing because Mr. Tyler didn't bother to question me.

"By all means." He waved his hand towards the door. "Just make sure to get notes from your friend there."

I gave Noah an apologetic smile and left the classroom. The ghost's loud voice followed me all the way down the hall.

Chapter 7

Lying to your teacher on the second day of school is not a good start, but neither is getting distracted by a lecturing ghost no one else could see or hear.

I decided I couldn't wait until after school to get that sage. If I hurried, I could be back in time before third period started. Luckily, the specialty store I'd found online was within walking distance from the school. I shoved my bag into my locker, made sure to put my wallet in my pocket and my phone in the other pocket, and slammed the door shut. It was loud while the halls were empty and everyone was in class.

I snuck out of the doors at the end of the hall closest to my locker and walked through a side yard to get to the sidewalk. No one stopped me.

As I headed towards the shop, I realized I would be walking right by the skatepark. For some reason, I grew excited for a second. Then I had to chide myself again.

What was wrong with me?

Brandon was a ghost. He might have been a cute, charming, and funny ghost, but he was still a ghost. There was no sense in continuing to talk to him. If anything, it would only hurt his focus on getting to the next stage or whatever happens after you die. Surely that's what ghosts were supposed to do, right? Work on going into the light or whatever? It seemed like talking to those who were still alive would be a distraction from finding that light.

I followed my line of thought and realized that even though I could see and talk to ghosts, I really didn't know much about them. Why were ghosts here anyway? A few movies I'd seen had said something about unfinished business. Brandon's unfinished business was surely not to hang out with me.

Yet I found myself looking for him as I walked by the fence that surrounded the skatepark. It was late morning, so no one was there. The kids were probably at school like I should have been. Any adults who might have used the park were probably also at work or sleeping in or something.

At first, I didn't see him. It was all empty cement with weeds growing through the cracks while wind blew through the slightly-too-tall green grass. I felt both relieved and disappointed.

Then I caught a glimpse of motion. The hairs on the back of my neck stood up, warning me of an impending ghost, and there he was, sitting alone in the grass, picking at a dandelion.

It would have been much easier to ignore him if he'd been busy skating, but there was something about seeing him alone in the grass that pulled at my heart. I was the only person he could talk to, and it looked like he'd been stuck there alone for at least twenty years, based off his choice of fashion. There didn't appear to be any other ghosts haunting the place, and even if there were, I'd never seen ghosts talk to each other. I'd been lonely a few times in my life and knew it wasn't a great feeling.

"Brandon?" I found myself saying, and I wasn't even scared. Points for me.

He whipped around to look at me so fast I worried he'd get whiplash. Ghosts probably don't get whiplash, you know, since they don't have bodies and all that.

"It's you!" He jumped up and ran to the fence. He didn't even hesitate or pause when he got to the metal and just went right through it. "I knew you'd be back."

"Oh, you did, eh? How did you know that?" I perked up a sassy eyebrow.

"With friends like you've got you must be as lonely as me."

It wasn't often that guys were so straightforward with their feelings and not embarrassed to admit something. He clearly was excited to see me, and he wasn't even trying to play it cool. It was admirable and refreshing.

It also made me want to hang with him, unworried about hiding my feelings since they were what they were. He certainly didn't seem too afraid of being himself, so why should I be?

"At least I've got friends."

He might have been right about my friends, but that didn't mean I couldn't banter back. His confidence with who he was and what he was feeling clued me in that he could take a bit of teasing.

"Yes, I sure wish someone would want to steal my math homework every day. Cheating really has a way of bringing people together, you know?"

I shook my head. "It's more like tutoring than cheating. Tutoring is a nice thing to do."

He studied me with an endearing side-smile. "Whatever you say, dear."

"I have a confession to make," I said, looking around to make sure no one was witnessing me chatting with a fence.

"Oh? Did you miss me? Don't worry. That's a usual response to my charm and sharp wits."

I rolled my eyes. "No. Talking to a ghost is the last thing I want to do, and I only talked to you because you looked so lonely over there. I'm headed to the store really quick before third period starts so I've got to hurry, but I'd thought I'd at least say hello."

"I don't mind being a charity case as long as it means I get to hang out with a girl as cute as you."

"Thank you? I think?"

"Anytime." He nodded like he was doing me a favor. "So where are we going?"

"We? We aren't going anywhere. You're a ghost, remember? You're stuck at your haunt. Ghosts can't travel."

"How do you know? I thought you didn't talk to ghosts."

"Which is another reason, even if you could travel, that you shouldn't be hanging out with me. It really isn't good to have a ghost follow me around. What would the other ghosts say?"

"Are you worried about the other ghosts or the alivers that might see you talking to a ghost?"

I sighed in exasperation. How did he understand me so well and so quickly? "Neither or both. Does it matter? You can't come with me anyway."

He shrugged. "Let's find out. Which way is the store?"

"That way." I pointed sullenly in the direction I'd been traveling but didn't feel too worried. There was no way he'd be able to go the whole way. It was just too far away from his haunt.

"Cool." He strode down the sidewalk, and I hurried to keep up with him.

"You can come with me, but you're just going to disappear after we pass the end of the fence. I want you to know I'm not sure when I'll be back, so I don't want you to be sitting and waiting for me, okay?"

"Just because I was sitting alone in the grass, not skating the perfectly good concrete, and picking at flowers, does not mean I was waiting for you." His side-smile never really left his face.

"Oh? What does it mean then?"

The fence post that marked the end of the skatepark was only a few paces away. I prepared myself for his imminent disappearance.

"It means that I was enjoying the feel of the sunshine on my back and the cool grass beneath my fingers, and that I was hoping someone good-looking and fun would walk by and talk to me."

"But you got me instead."

"Exactly. See? Not missing you or waiting for you to come back at all."

I grinned as we passed the pole. "Well, see you around."

But he didn't disappear. He kept walking next to me with confidence and attitude. "You were saying?"

I glanced back at the skatepark and pulled my eyebrows together. "That's weird. How are you doing this? A ghost has never followed me so far before."

He shrugged as if it were no big deal. Maybe it wasn't to him, but if ghosts could follow me away from their haunts, I truly would be haunted for the rest of my life. That was something that I just couldn't deal with. I'd never feel peace again. People would notice how distracted I'd be, and I'd end up a crazy cat lady or something—possibly even one of those homeless people with wild hair who always talked to themselves, or at least that's what it would look like from the living people's point of view.

The crushing fear of constantly being followed by several ghosts completely pushed out the concern of being back at school in time for the next class. I felt my chest tighten, and I had to work hard to even breathe.

"You don't understand. If you can follow me around past your haunt, that means other ghosts can too. Do you know how many ghosts there are?" I glanced around the quiet suburban houses in the daytime, again looking for ghosts or people who might see what was going on.

All seemed clear, so far.

Brandon held up his hands in a calming motion. "Woah, there. Take a breath. It's just you and me right now. There aren't any other ghosts here. I'm sorry to make you so upset. You're right. I don't understand."

I breathed heavily and ran fingers through my hair, completely undoing any earlier efforts I'd made to keep it from being wild. "This cannot be happening."

"I'd offer to disappear for you, but I'm afraid that's outside my skill level right now. Let's back up a bit, okay?"

I nodded and tried to focus on slowing my breathing.

"There are rules to being a ghost. One of them is that a ghost is stuck in one place and cannot leave their haunt, correct?"

Again, I nodded.

"This is the first time you've seen a ghost travel outside of their haunt?"

I almost nodded but paused. "Er—well, yes, except my grandma. She's the only ghost I've seen that can haunt a person. She follows my mom everywhere."

"That's heartbreaking." Brandon placed his hands on his chest in sympathy. I could see both through his hands and his chest. The sidewalk looked misty and blue behind him. "But is she like trying to hurt her and make scary things happen in order to communicate or something?"

"Not yet. So far, she's just like my grandma was when she was alive. She worries about my mom and tries to give her advice all the time. Of course, my mom can't hear her, but my grandma still tries anyway." I felt calmer as we talked through things logically, but the waves of panic were still roaring under the surface, ready to splurge over the shore if another ghost showed up.

"Have any other ghosts been following your mom around since your grandma died?"

"I haven't seen one, but that's different. My mom can't see or talk to ghosts. I can, and once a ghost figures that out, they don't leave me alone. Case in point." I gestured my arm up and down at him.

He grinned. "Yes, but none are as awesome as me. Shall we continue your walk to the store? We can hash this out as we go. I have complete confidence that you'll be just fine."

I checked the time on my phone and saw that third period was going to start in ten minutes. I was definitely not going to make it, but I might as well do what I had set out to do. There was no way I could spend another day in history class trying not to listen to that ghost. He was just too loud.

"Fine, but you've got to do me a favor. If we see other people or other ghosts, even just one other ghost, you've got to stop talking to me. None of those funny side comments or chatty conversations. Otherwise, things will get bad for me, got it?"

I pointed my finger in his face, so he'd understand how important it was.

He pretended to nip at my finger with a grin. "Got it."

"Good." I turned and headed towards the store.

"It occurs to me that you gave me permission to come with you. Do you remember what you said?" Brandon easily kept stride with me and put his hands in his pocket. The chain on his pants swung with his leg as we walked down the sidewalk. I could almost hear the clink of the metal.

"I did say you could come with me."

He nodded. "Yup, and at that moment I felt a little tingle of power. It could have been the tingles I get when talking to pretty girls, but I think this one was a little different."

"Oh, like when you said you could feel my power yesterday while we were sitting at the tables? Perhaps you're on to something. Do you think all the ghosts can feel my power?"

"Not sure. I'm just one ghost, and I have no idea what the other ghosts go through. All I know is that once you reacted to me, it was if a connection had formed, and I could feel some kind of pull towards you."

"Hmm. It would at least explain why ghosts start to swarm me if I acknowledge only one. I'm going to say that the others can feel it, too."

"But only after you do something to react. Like for me, you winced when I fell."

"Right. Interesting."

"See? It's not so bad. Just ignore them like you've been doing, and they won't notice your power."

"But what about interacting with you in front of another ghost. Will that break the barrier?"

He shrugged. "Dunno."

"You're so helpful."

"Hey, we've figured out this much so far. From what I can tell, that's progress for you, Miss Completely-Ignore-Your-Awesome-Powers."

I frowned but didn't know how to respond to that.

"So where are we going, anyway? What kind of shopping do you need to do during school hours? It must be something important. Oh!" He looked around and lowered his voice. "Is it for... you know... lady things?"

I swatted at him, but of course my hand passed through his shoulder. We both pretended not to notice. "No! It's for sage. I need special organic white sage to get rid of a ghost that's haunting my history class. We've only had two days of school, but already he's driving me crazy!"

"And this special sage is supposed to...?"

"I read on the internet that it can help get rid of ghosts or unwanted spirits and this guy is definitely unwanted."

"Poor guy. It's not fun to feel unwanted."

"It's not fun either to try and listen to people who are actually alive when a dead guy is practically yelling a lecture about Abraham Lincoln. I have got to get into a good college and history is one of my favorite classes. I cannot fail!"

Brandon held his hands up in surrender. "Alright. Yes, you need to get rid of him, and using sage is supposed to do that? Seems a bit too easy, don't you think? Have you tried just asking him to go away?"

I glared. "And like just asking him to go away isn't too easy? You know what happens when I talk to ghosts. Look at what happened when I talked to you. Now you won't go away."

"That stings, but you get a pass because I know you love having me around." He batted his eyelashes prettily.

After walking past a few houses that gave way to a more commercial part of town, we arrived at the store. It looked like a house had been turned into a business. There was a big sign sitting in the yard out front with the palm of a hand and an eye staring out from the palm. It read "Psychic Services and Shop". On one side of the house was a quiet, cute coffee and book shop I would have much rather gone into. On the other side was your standard dry-cleaning store.

Since it was early in the day, there weren't many people going about their business, and by the looks of the psychic house, I wondered if it was even going to be open. I should have checked when it opened before ditching school.

Too late now.

Brandon stood next to me as we appraised the building. "I can already tell that being your friend is going to take me on lots of fun adventures. I'll be living my life finally. It's just ironic that I'm already dead before I'd finally get to live."

"Alright, Socrates, let's just see if it's open. All I need is some high-quality sage, and we can get back out here into the sunshine."

I walked a few paces towards the house but stopped abruptly and pointed at him again. "Remember, be quiet! Do not make me laugh. It's just rude, and I don't want to look more insane than I already do."

"Yeah, your hair is kind of messed up."

I huffed and tried to smooth it out with my fingers. "Ugh, you're terrible."

He grinned and used a zipping motion across his lips to indicate he was going to be quiet.

Chapter 8

Relieved that the store appeared to be operational, I opened the door and a bell jingled to signal my entrance.

"Come in! I'll be there in a moment!" A faint voice threaded to us from somewhere in the back.

The store was a mess. It was so dimly lit, my eyes took a few seconds to adjust. I didn't know much about owning a store, but I did figure that a clean and more organized space would be easier for guests to find what they needed, and thereby, have a better experience. Clearly this person wasn't worried about any of that.

Stuff was everywhere. I could see where bookshelves lined the walls, but they were so packed and full that it was difficult to see them. There were books, to be sure, but there was much more than that—weird jars full of floating items I didn't want to take a closer look at, piles of leaves or grass or something, baskets full of multi-colored clothes with insane patterns, dried flowers hanging upside down from any free ceiling space, and several mismatched tables of trinkets and accessories and crystals. It was overwhelming after the quiet of the sunshiny afternoon.

Incense burned behind the counter that I assumed was the cash register because there was a small, cleared space and a computer.

"Now this would be a haunt. Much cooler than a stupid skatepark," Brandon said as we looked around.

I glared at him for talking, but he just flashed me that stupidly charming grin.

Carefully, we made our way around the shop. My eyes were drawn to the piles of leaves and plants, and I would have tried to sort through them, but I realized I'd had no idea what sage even looked like.

"Ah, excuse me. Welcome to Rose's Psychictry and Shop," a tall woman said as she emerged from a beaded curtain leading to another room. Her appearance was completely at odds with the shop around us. Her light hair was pulled tightly into a bun on the top of her head. She wore a simple white blouse and stylish, well-fitting jeans with holes in them. She did have some funky purple glasses with large beads glued to the frames, but that was the oddest bit about her. Even her face was done up with tasteful makeup.

"Is Psychictry even a real word?" Brandon eyed the lady dubiously.

"I'm Rose. How can I help you?" She wore a smile as she walked into the room, but as she got a look at me, her manicured brows furrowed slightly, and she looked around as if expecting to see more people.

Working hard not to glance at Brandon, I put on a friendly smile and took a few more steps inside the shop. "Hi, Rose. My name is Hanna. I won't take much of your time. I'm just looking for some organic white sage."

Rose studied me for a moment, but her customer-service smile never left her face.

"Er—do you carry organic white sage? I looked it up online and saw this was the closest place." I looked around the shop, hoping to pull her into motion with my curiosity.

I could have sworn she looked right at Brandon for a second. He felt her gaze enough to stiffen his back and glance at me. I made sure not to look in his direction. Was it possible she could see ghosts, too?

She returned to Earth and gestured to a shelf on my left. "Of course, I carry it. What kind of place wouldn't carry white sage?"

I expected a snarky comment from Brandon, but he looked too unnerved to speak, and I doubted it was because I'd told him to be quiet.

"Right." I chuckled politely.

It wasn't difficult for her to stretch up to the tallest shelf and pull out a white basket full of grey leaves and stalks, some bundled together with string.

"I have plenty of sage, but I'm pretty sure that's not going to take care of your problem."

She weaved through the tables and headed towards the cashier counter. I followed behind her. Brandon and I shared a wide-eyed look while her back was turned.

"It'll be fine. How much for a bundle of it? Is there any special way that I should wave it around?"

She bent under the counter for a second and came back up with a simple brown bag. "Messing with spirits is no game. Are you sure you know what you're doing?"

I nodded confidently. "Oh, I know. Some would say it's life and death. Two bundles would probably do it."

Her lips twitched slightly at my dumb joke. "It depends on the space you need to cleanse, and the type of negativity you feel there, of course. Again, I'm not sure white sage is strong enough for what you need."

"I have a plan. How much for two bundles?" I pulled my wallet from my back pocket. "Do you take cards?"

Rose's grey, almost purple eyes, never left my face as she placed two bundles into the bag. "A plan, eh? What if it goes wrong?"

"Then I have a few more steps I can try." I tried to keep the smile on my face, but my patience and confidence was wavering. How much could she know about what I needed? She seemed so sure of herself.

She pursed her lips together and then seemed to make a decision. "Alright. We'll try it your way. That'll be ten dollars. When it doesn't work, you can come back, and then we'll get started on the real work."

Feeling petulant, I handed her my card, but I didn't know what else to say to reassure her. She didn't know me.

Apparently, she could take cards because she took the plastic from me and ran it through a slider on her phone. She tapped a few times and handed the card back. Our hands accidentally made skin contact for a second. I say accidentally because it would have been weird if she'd done it on purpose, but I couldn't have been sure.

Her eyes widened when we touched. Even her smile faded just a little bit. Cheeks flushing, I put the card back into my wallet and shoved it into the back pocket of my jeans.

"Thank you so much!" I grabbed the bag from her hands before she even extended it towards me and walked quickly out of the store. I didn't even wait to see if Brandon followed, figuring he could handle himself.

"See you tomorrow!" Rose called out as the door shut and I escaped back into the world of sunlight.

Brandon skipped down the sidewalk next to me while I walked so fast, I almost broke into a run.

"Quit laughing at me!"

He stopped a chuckle, but the grin was still there. "If I didn't know better, I'd say you were scared of that lady."

My pace slowed some as we headed back towards the skatepark and school. "Didn't she give you the creeps? Couldn't you feel that weirdness she had? She might need to burn a little sage in her own shop."

"If you have any left over, you could stop by tomorrow and cleanse the place for her. I'm sure she'd appreciate that."

"I know you felt it. She looked right at you, and you got quiet. She can see ghosts, too."

Brandon shrugged. "It was creepy in the moment, but out here in the daylight, it doesn't seem that big a deal. She is a psychic, right? That's what they do?"

I shook my head, trying to clear my mind. "It just seems weird. That's all."

"You didn't think you were the only special person in the world, did you?"

I rolled my eyes. "Of course not. I'm just saying it freaked me out. I'm allowed to be freaked out, right?"

His smile changed to a more sympathetic one. "Of course. I didn't mean to be rude. Just teasing."

"And don't think I've forgotten how you kept talking even when I told you to be quiet." I waved my finger again, so he'd know I wasn't too upset.

"It's difficult to silence genius, but I do understand how important it is to you. I'll try to do better."

"I appreciate that."

"So now where are we going? Back to school?"

"What? You're going to come back with me to school?" My heartbeat rose, but I wasn't sure if it was because I wanted him to come with me or I didn't. Emotions are confusing sometimes.

He shrugged. "What else do I have to do? The only way I can travel is by hanging out with you. Aren't you lucky?"

"Er—sure." I frowned. "It's not that I don't like you or don't want you around, it's just—"

"I stink?"

"Yes, your smell that I can't smell because you're a ghost is disgusting. Can you please take a shower at least once a year?"

"It's true that I haven't had one in quite a while. Perhaps I could borrow yours?"

I had to stop that line of thought immediately. "No. Absolutely not. Go find a river somewhere. It's not just your smell, you're invisible, and I really don't need a ghost following me around, complicating my life."

We were in front of the skatepark by then and it was still empty. I felt bad leaving him there, but I didn't have a choice. The last thing I needed was a ghost hanging around all the time, no matter how funny or cute he was.

He frowned and kicked at a pebble. It didn't move, of course. "I understand. Life is busy and a ghost would just get in the way. You probably have lots of ghosts who want to talk with you. It gets quite lonely as a ghost and having someone to talk to is very nice."

I sighed. "I'm sorry. Thank you for understanding. I'll try to come visit you soon. Okay?"

He didn't look like he believed me as I walked away, even after I gave him an encouraging wave.

I did feel bad; I did. But I just did not have enough room in my head to handle everything that was going on and him, too. It's important to know your limits, you know?

Also, what if while I was trying to get rid of the teacher ghost, I got rid of Brandon, too? It was the first time in my life I wasn't sure I wanted to get rid of a ghost. How weird is that?

I'll answer for you. Weird.

Chapter 9

I made it back to school during the end of third period. I had missed my second class of history and English. Not a great start to the year. Hopefully I could get back on track. I wasn't a perfect student, but I still wanted to get good grades. Even though I didn't know what I wanted to do after high school yet, I did know it was important to do my best in school.

Art class went by quickly, mostly because I was preoccupied with how I was going to use the sage and clean the classroom. I obviously couldn't do it during school hours. The time after school before they locked up for the night would probably work, but only if Mr. Tyler didn't hang out in his classroom all evening. Perhaps I could use a distraction to get him out for a few minutes, but who could I get to help me?

Before lunch, I stopped by my locker and put my books away. The sage was tucked safely in the corner of my upper shelf and gave off a light smell. Maybe it wouldn't hurt to keep the sage around with me all the time. Even if I managed to get rid of the teacher ghost, my haunting problems were far from over.

My body felt slightly shaky from not having much food in the last two days, but I didn't want to ruin the progress I had made by eating something unhealthy and fattening. It was a lot harder to lose weight than to gain it.

I grabbed a bottle of water and an apple. The cafeteria ghost was there again, and I worried that my mere presence was enough to make her stronger. It seemed that the teacher ghost had gotten stronger, and after talking with Brandon, I worried what kind of effects I had on the other ghosts. The last thing I wanted was to see them more and have them stick around just because there was something broken inside of me.

Our table was full of my friends and the friends of my friends. As I walked towards them, Noah scooted over and patted the seat next to him. Andrea was sitting across the table and her eyes narrowed so much I wasn't even sure they were still open. Randi raised her eyebrows and her wide eyes darted between Andrea and Noah.

"Hey, I saved you a seat." Noah's smile was friendly, and I wasn't sure if he was ignoring Andrea or just clueless.

I didn't want to make Andrea mad but there was no way I could refuse the invitation. Noah was a big boy; he could make his own decisions.

"Thank you." I nestled in between him and Stephanie. The fit was so close, my forearm brushed against Noah's and the contact sent thrills through me.

So, sue me—I'm a sucker for even a little attention.

"Did you get lost, again?" Stephanie greeted me with a teasing smile. She also had blonde hair like Andrea's, but it was straight and long, like down to the small of her back long.

"Nah. I just like to make an entrance." I returned her smile, so she knew I wasn't trying to be stuck up.

Andrea rolled her eyes. "Or she had to poop."

Giggles erupted around the table and even Noah chuckled. Given their response and the fact that I had already made Andrea angry, I chose to roll with it. What was the harm? Everyone poops, right?

"When you gotta go, you gotta go." I shrugged nonchalantly.

This time the laughter bothered Andrea even more, if looking at her glaring expression was any indication. Oops. I couldn't ever seem to do the right thing around her.

"How are you feeling? Did your migraine go away already?" Noah asked as the others returned to their various, separate conversations. Andrea's eyes never left Noah's face even though Alex was next to her and was trying to ask her a question about a class they had together.

I twisted the cap off my water bottle and took a quick swig before answering him. He wasn't supposed to notice my odd behavior, but I had announced in front of the whole class that I was going to puke. "Oh, it was just a small headache. I feel fine now. What did I miss?"

Just as Noah started explaining the discussion they'd had in history class, I noticed Caleb and Trina's group of friends heading towards us. Trina trailed right behind Caleb with a curious expression.

"Hey, guys. How's it going?" Caleb flashed his white smile at my group of friends and most of the girls visibly wilted.

Stephanie was the first to recover. "It's good. Y'all need a place to sit?"

Trina appraised the table. "I don't think there's room here. Let's go to our usual spot. Caleb?"

His dark eyes didn't even glance at Trina. "We'd love to sit with you guys. Do you mind if I scoot right in here?"

He gestured at the space between Stephanie and me.

"Of course!" Stephanie eagerly shooed off a few disgruntled acquaintances at the end of the table who weren't finished eating their lunches.

Everyone shuffled down the bench enough to let Caleb's broad shoulders have space. The rest of Trina's friends filtered into the empty spots. Trina gave me a weird look from the end of the table but the whole situation was so odd, I didn't know how to interpret it. What was happening? Why did this sexy group of seniors want to sit with us?

Then I happened to glance at Noah and the anger sparking out of his eyes was stronger than Andrea's had been just a moment before. As for Andrea, she looked pleased with the attention.

"What are you doing here?" Noah glared at Caleb over the top of my head.

"Do you guys know each other?" I asked, glancing between both.

While Noah looked like he could cook eggs with his laser glare, Caleb looked as comfortable as if he were sitting by the beach sipping Kool-Aid.

"How do *you* know him?" Noah turned his heated glare onto me, and it lessened only slightly.

Why did I suddenly feel like I was on trial for doing something wrong?

"He's friends with my sister." I gestured towards Trina with my thumb. She paused in taking a bite of potato chip to give him a polite smile.

"Of course he is."

I gave him an odd look, but I didn't want to poke the beast anymore. Obviously, he didn't like Caleb but other than the fact that he was reasonable competition in the looks department, I had no idea why.

Andrea, on the other hand, was unable to stay away from the drama. Her eyes looked Noah up and down. "How *do* you know him?"

"Noah and I are on the football team together, that's all. No biggie." Caleb shrugged, perhaps trying to ease the tension.

"Well, *I* don't know you," Stephanie said from Caleb's other side. "But I think I'd like to."

Trina rolled her eyes and Caleb chuckled. "My name is Caleb. Like Little Sanchez here said, I'm friends with her sister, Trina. I figured we're all like one big family, and just wanted to get to know y'all."

"Sure, you do," Noah muttered quietly as he poked his instant mashed potatoes with a fork.

"I didn't know you had a sister, Hanna," Randi said, staring at Caleb with a dreamy look in her eyes as she played with a curl of her dark hair.

"You don't talk about how awesome I am to your friends?" Trina huffed playfully. "How rude."

Andrea studied the two of us. "You two look nothing alike."

"Yeah, Trina is more clearly the supermodel of the two of us." I plastered a teasing smile on my face, so people didn't think I was being too serious or bitter.

"Clearly." Andrea smirked.

"They're both beautiful in their own ways." Caleb nodded to each of us.

Trina shook her head, amused, but I blushed furiously.

The attention was too much for me, so I turned back to Noah to resume our conversation. I really did need to know about our history class. "What were you saying about history? What did we do in class?"

Noah glanced at Caleb over my head, but I couldn't read his expression. I just knew it wasn't friendly. "Right. We discussed different points of view on the same story. He brought out different newspaper articles about the same situation and we compared them."

"He's the weirdest history teacher I've ever had." I shook my head, aware that several people were listening in on our conversation. Some had gone back to their own conversations, but Andrea and Caleb's listening ears felt like weights. "It's starting out more like a journalism class than history."

Noah nodded and his shoulders relaxed slightly. "But I like the discussion style better than the other teacher's. Sitting in a lecture is so boring."

"Tell me about it." Remembering the lecturing ghost, I cringed.

I had figured out why I needed to be in Mr. Tyler's classroom after school. I just needed to figure out how to be in there alone for long enough to do some kind of weird sage cleansing dance. It occurred to me that I might need a lookout, but no one living would do.

"Sounds like you guys have Mr. Tyler for history," Caleb said after taking a sip of Coke.

"I have him, too, for fifth period." Andrea picked at her nails to appear nonchalant, but it was unlike her to pay attention so much to my conversations. "Did you have him sophomore year, Caleb?"

"Oh yeah, most of us did. He was a good teacher, but there was something off about the classroom. I can't explain it, but I felt a bit of a weird presence in there or something. Do you know what I mean?" Caleb looked right at me, even though he had been answering a question of Andrea's.

"Er—no? Are you saying the classroom is haunted?" I forced a laugh and looked to my friends to back me up.

Andrea's eyebrow rose, but she didn't join in my laughter. Noah gave another scathing look at Caleb, and the whole exchange confirmed that I had no idea what was really going on.

Was it possible that Caleb could see ghosts, too?

I know. It sounds so dumb. Regular people can feel bad spirits and auras, too. He could have been more intuitive than others.

But then, why had he looked right at me when he'd said that?

Thankfully, the tension eased throughout the rest of lunch. Andrea and Noah went back to talking about people they knew from cheer and football. Randi and Stephanie kept Caleb busy by asking him lots of questions about what being a senior was like. Trina kept herself busy talking to her other friends, and I fiddled with my apple until the bell rang.

For the next three classes, my mind kept returning to Mr. Tyler's classroom. I finally had a tentative plan when we got to math. Andrea sat next to me, and I smelled a whiff of perfume, the expensive kind. I wondered if she sprayed it on herself between every class or just every other class. It took work to keep up that much aroma. My perfume usually wore off thirty minutes after I'd applied it, and my foundation wasn't far behind.

Mr. Mink had us exchange papers, and we graded our answers together. I had been wrong about question seven, but I'd gotten all the others correct.

Andrea had my paper and I had hers, naturally. Without hesitation, she fixed the answer instead of marking it wrong and gave me a pointed look. I smiled at her weakly and also fixed the answer. It had been my fault she'd gotten it wrong, anyway. She might have gotten it right had she done it herself, so fixing it was the least I could do.

I'm aware of how I sound, thank you very much.

Being friends with Andrea and the crew was more important to me than marking a problem wrong.

After Mr. Mink went over the material for the day and assigned us another worksheet, I turned to Andrea as we packed up. "Do you want to meet in the skatepark again to work on math?"

She looked her phone and frowned. "Not tonight. We can just meet up at lunch tomorrow. That will give you more time to make sure the answers are right."

"Okay." I put my pencil into the front pocket of my bag. "Wasn't it so weird that Trina and her friends showed up at lunch today? I wonder if that will be a whole thing or what."

"That was odd. Caleb must be hunting for fresh blood, figuring us gullible sophomores wouldn't notice he's on the prowl."

"Oh, do you think he's a player like that? He seemed kind of nice and genuine to me."

"That's because you're a gullible sophomore, sweetie." She flashed her teeth in what was supposed to be a smile and exited the classroom with a whoosh of perfume.

Chapter 10

Despite not needing to meet Andrea at the skatepark after school, I went straight that way anyway. Brandon was the only other person—are ghosts considered persons or things? I'll say person. He was the only person who knew my situation and even though he was a ghost, and I was trying to avoid them, I knew he'd be the best candidate to help me.

Plus, going to the skatepark to pick him up would give the school time to clear out for the day. I just needed to get back before Mr. Tyler left his classroom and locked up or I would have a whole other hurdle to jump.

The park was much busier than it had been during the late morning. Skaters were zipping and zooming all over the place while others stood and watched or chatted in the grass. Brandon was nowhere in sight.

"Brandon?" I said, careful not to call loudly or draw attention to myself. "Where are you? I know you're here. You can't go anywhere else."

Cold air prickled the hairs on the back of my neck, and I whirled around to see him grinning at me, hands in his gigantic pockets. "Did you miss me already?"

"Hardly." I glanced around to see if anyone was watching me talk to myself. "I need your help. Time for a second field trip."

"I love field trips!" He practically skipped next to me as I walked out of the park and onto the sidewalk.

"I figured you would, but this one comes with a job. We're not going out for fun. I'm putting you to work. If I have to put up with you, at least I should get something out of it."

"You mean more than just pure enjoyment from my company? I suppose that's fair."

I gave him a side-eye. "Right. As enjoyable as that is, I need more."

"Girls always do."

"Because I'm sure you know so much about girls hanging out with a bunch of skater boys all day."

"Hey, I had a sister and a mother and..." he trailed off as he stared at our feet.

My heart sank and I felt terrible. Why hadn't I thought about that before? Of course Brandon had had a life before this. I was just so used to ghosts in my current time, that I rarely thought much about their lives before they died.

"I'm sorry. I didn't mean to bring up the past like that." I wasn't sure what the right words were, but I did know an apology seemed appropriate.

He shrugged. "I know you didn't. What year is it?"

I told him.

"Yikes! Where are all the hover cars and cool body suits? Such a disappointment."

I smiled. "Yeah, those aren't here yet, but you'll be surprised to see what we've done with computers and the internet. So? What year did you die?"

"Oh, 1999."

"Can I ask what happened?"

"You can ask, but that doesn't mean I'll tell you."

"Fair enough."

We walked together in silence until we were three houses away from the school parking lot.

"Alright, here's the plan. I'm going to get into the classroom and my sage. If Mr. Tyler is in the room, I'll make up some excuse about why he needs to leave for a bit."

"Like what?"

"I don't know. I'll think of something. Hopefully the door will be wide open with no live people in sight, and it won't be an issue."

"Right… so you don't have much of a plan. Can you even call this a plan? It's more like a pl—you know, the P L without the A N."

I rolled my eyes. "So, after he leaves, I'll wave the sage all over, careful not to have any interaction with the ghost."

"It's possible that doing this cleanse will be enough to count as interaction with the ghost. For me, all you had to do was wince and I could feel your focus. Have you tried talking to the guy, yet? He might not even realize he's dead."

"I am *not* talking to him. Like I said, I don't need another one of you to follow me around."

"You mean to help you on weird plans that aren't very good? To provide you with great, real-time, commentary on the world around us? I'm your own personal narrator. Who else can say that?"

"Has anyone told you you're a bit full of yourself?" I slowed my pace as we neared the side doors of the school. The parking lot had nearly emptied out and only a few students were milling about.

"Confidence is sexy."

"So is actually having a body."

"Rude."

I reached for the door and pulled it open. The smell of bleach and old carpet whooshed out to greet us. "Your only job is to keep watch. Stay further down the hallway so you don't accidentally get cleansed with the sage, but close enough that you can see if anyone is coming towards the classroom. All you have to do is shout a warning if someone is coming. You can even be as loud as you want since no one else will hear you. Isn't that neat?"

"The neatest."

We walked through the mostly empty hallways. A few students were leaving the building or talking in small groups. I hoped Mr. Tyler wouldn't be in his room, but that the door would still be open.

I got lucky that one of those things was true. As we turned down the 40s hallway, I was relieved to see the light spilling out of his classroom with the door open. We could hear voices talking, and as we got closer, they got louder. Some of the other classroom doors were also open, but a few were closed and dark.

"This school hasn't changed a bit," Brandon noted as we walked towards Mr. Tyler's room.

Although it was stupid for being surprised, I was surprised. Of course, he'd gone to school here. He had probably lived nearby and spent lots of time at the skatepark. Why else would that be his haunt?

I didn't respond, though, because I didn't want to be talking to myself in public, again.

I stopped and pointed to the wall several paces away from Mr. Tyler's room in what I hoped would be far enough that the sage wouldn't bother him. Brandon got the hint and gave me an encouraging thumbs up as he leaned against the wall to be my lookout.

"You bring up a good point," Mr. Tyler said as I peered around the door and into his room. "But that's not how everyone saw it."

He was talking to a student I didn't recognize. She was tall with short brown hair and was wearing a t-shirt and basketball shorts. One of those athletic bags that cinched at the top was slung over her shoulder. They were standing by his desk, but when Mr. Tyler saw me peek in, he waved me over.

"And how did everyone see it? It's so obvious—" the girl trailed off as she saw me entering the room. I wasn't sure if she was just being polite to pause the conversation or if she didn't want me to hear what she was going to say next.

Whatever she was thinking, it was awkward. I kept back a few paces to signify that I wasn't trying to butt into their conversation and that they could finish up. It gave me a few seconds to figure out how to get alone with the ghost. He hadn't shown up yet, but I knew he was around.

"Why don't you write a short essay about it?" Mr. Tyler continued to the girl. "If you can find both sides to the story, I'll give you extra credit."

She sighed. "That doesn't sound fun."

"You might be surprised how fun it is to look at one situation from different sides. Plus, extra credit would be nice to have come exam time."

"I guess."

"Think about how smart you'll look when we talk about it in class tomorrow," Mr. Tyler said with a teasing grin.

She gave a faint smile as she rolled her eyes. "We'll see. Later."

They waved at each other as she left. She didn't give me another look as she passed by.

Mr. Tyler turned his bright blue eyes on me. "I'm glad to see you're feeling better. You are feeling better, right? I don't enjoy having vomit on my carpet. The smell lingers."

I cringed. "Sounds like you know from experience."

"Even high school students have normal bodily functions. Unfortunately, throwing up happens to be one of those. Has your migraine gone away?"

I rubbed at my head, hoping I looked convincing. "Oh, yes. I'm here to apologize for having to leave class, and I wanted to get the notes from the lesson today."

He turned to his desk and shuffled around some papers. "I don't usually hand out lecture notes to students. Don't you have a friend you can get the notes from? When you go to college, you'll find professors don't take any responsibility for classes you miss. That's all on you."

As he was talking, it was just my luck that the ghost teacher took that moment to arrive. He fazed in through the wall and was, thankfully, reading a book. I really needed to get Mr. Tyler out of the room.

"I know. I'm sorry." I pulled my eyes from the ghost and focused on Mr. Tyler. He had been busy looking on his desk, so he hadn't seen my eyes wander. "I do have a friend in class, Noah Jenkins. We sat next to each other today."

Mr. Tyler looked at me over the top of his bifocals. "Oh, right. Didn't you get notes from him?"

"I totally would have, but he's a terrible note taker. He probably just doodled pictures of pizza during class. I want to make sure I start out the year doing well in here. Are you sure you can't give me a copy of the lecture notes? I'm sure you come prepared to class with a detailed plan of what you want to talk about."

"Flattery will not work on me, Sanchez. Lucky for you, I do have a soft spot for students who actually care about getting good grades. Let me go make a copy of this for you." He waved a paper that he'd picked up from the pile.

Relief poured over me and was probably evident all over my face. "Oh, thank you! I'll wait here."

Mr. Tyler left the classroom, and I heard Brandon call out from the hall, "The eagle has left the nest."

I fished the sage out of my bag and grabbed the box of matches I'd stolen from our kitchen. As I lit the match and started burning the sage, I realized that it could set the fire alarm off. That wouldn't be good.

When the sage was smoldering enough that it wouldn't go out with movement, I began to wave it around the room. I started in the back where Mr. Tyler's desk was and made some zigzags and circles. I tried to spread it all through the air, past the bookshelves and between the aisles of the desks and chairs—avoiding the fire detector as well as I could. As I approached the front of the room, the ghost teacher looked up from his book, and I was certain to not make eye contact.

He put the book down on some invisible desk and it disappeared. "What are you doing here after hours?"

Pressing my lips to keep focus, I kept waving the sage, making a big show of trying to get it all over the room. After the desks, I started in the right corner and reached up as high as I could, and then bent down low to get near the floor. I repeated the process all through the front of the classroom.

The worst part was when I neared the ghost. I saved his spot for last, which is probably breaking the rules of acknowledgement, but I wanted the sage to be all over the place so he would have nowhere to hide.

"Excuse me! What are you doing?" The ghost backed up a couple of steps as I waved the sage in his direction. "You're acting like a lunatic. Are you some kind of witch? You aren't one of my students!"

It disappointed me that he was able to step back into the space that I had already cleansed. I was also disappointed that he wasn't wavering or disappearing at all. I worried that I wasn't doing it right and inched closer towards him.

"Get that out of my face!" The ghost waved his hand through the burning sage as I focused more on his position. "Are you listening to me, girl? Stop what you're doing, immediately!"

And that's when a real book hit me in the shoulder.

I gasped and dropped the sage. It landed on the carpet, still smoldering steadily. "Ouch!"

"I told you to stop!" the ghost said, picked up another, very real book, and brandished it about. "Quit putting that weird weed in my face. If you don't get out of my classroom right now, I'm going to call the police and have you committed!"

"The eagle is flying home, and he's coming in quickly. Also, that sage tickles my nose." Brandon called down the hall. His voice echoed, and the ghost teacher looked up at the words. I wasn't the only one that could hear Brandon.

I had assumed that ghosts could hear each other, but I'd never witnessed them interacting before. I was learning all kinds of things from hanging out with Brandon.

"Do you have a friend out there? I'll have you both expelled for such odd behavior." The ghost lobbed another book, but I was smart enough to dodge it that time.

Quickly, I stamped out the sage and shoved it into my backpack. There were charred pieces of plant in the carpet, but I was relieved that the heat hadn't done any permanent damage. It also, apparently, hadn't done anything to cleanse the ghost. Instead, I was being pummeled by books, too shocked to consider why the ghost was suddenly able to interact with the physical world.

Mr. Tyler strolled into the classroom as another book went sailing. I had taken cover under a row of desks and chairs, and poor, unsuspecting Mr. Tyler got a book to the shoulder, or he would have, if he hadn't had the reflexes of a motion detector. He dodged it just in time.

"Hey! What's going on?" Mr. Tyler looked around the room in alarm.

"Who are you? Get out of my classroom!" The ghost grabbed another book from one of the two bookshelves in the front of the room. The shelves were filled with old history textbooks, giving him plenty of ammunition.

Mr. Tyler ducked again, and his speed gave me pause. It wasn't often that I'd seen anyone move that fast, especially not an older person. I supposed Mr. Tyler was more fit than I had given him credit for.

He finally noticed I was hiding underneath a desk, and books continued to fly over our heads as he crawled over to sit next to me.

"What did you do to the ghost?" Mr. Tyler peered over the desk and ducked as another book sailed overhead.

"I didn't mean to make him so mad! I was just trying to cleanse the room. Wait—how did you know there was a ghost?"

Brandon must have gotten curious about the yelling and thudding, and he peeked his head into the room. "What's going on? Oi!"

"Ah, the accomplice! You will both be expelled from school! Your college dreams are over, my boy! Might as well enlist immediately," said the teacher ghost and he threw several papers in Brandon's direction. They fanned out and fluttered to the ground like falling leaves in autumn.

Mr. Tyler looked confused for a moment as papers reigned in the opposite direction, but I didn't stop to explain.

"I've always known this classroom was haunted, but it's never been this bad. I've never seen it ever move anything. Did you make it stronger, somehow?" Mr. Tyler's blue eyes studied me as we crouched underneath the desk.

"I'm not sure. I didn't mean to. I was just trying to cleanse the room. I'm so sorry!" I swallowed, not allowing myself to cry.

"Let's get out of here and give it time to calm down. Head towards the door, but don't get hit by the books."

"Sounds good."

The teacher ghost was still hollering and chucking books. Papers flew around in mini tornadoes.

Crouching, I headed straight for the door. My thighs burned before I made it, but luckily, I wasn't hit with another book.

"Get out of my classroom! You aren't a student here! You belong in an asylum!" The ghost teacher hollered.

I could still hear him behind the door as Mr. Tyler shut and locked it. One last book hit it with a loud *thunk*, and I couldn't help but wince.

"So much for your plan." Brandon arched his eyebrow.

I glared but was grateful for the anger. It was much better to be angry than sobbing like a wussy baby. "That's not what was supposed to happen."

"And what was supposed to happen?" Mr. Tyler asked, assuming I had been talking to him.

I mean, who else would I have been talking to? Another ghost? Of course not!

"Right. I was cleansing the room with sage. I had thought, well, hoped, actually, that it would get rid of the ghost."

"Guess you proved that theory wrong. What's the next step on your list?" Brandon asked.

I was getting better at ignoring him while others were around, sort of.

Mr. Tyler scratched his white, trimmed beard. "Why did you think sage would get rid of him? Have you actually gotten rid of a ghost with sage before? I've never heard of that working."

"It was just a suggestion I saw. What have you heard of working?"

"Mr. Teacher here seems to be pretty comfortable talking about ghosts." Brandon scrunched his eyes as if he could pry out all the secrets with just a look.

"Why is it so important to you to get rid of this ghost? Up until now, he's just been a cold spot that washes through me once in a while. He's never been angry or able to pick up anything as far as I can tell. By the way, how do you know it's even a he?"

Brandon was right about one thing. It was odd that Mr. Tyler seemed so comfortable chatting about ghosts in an empty hallway after having just been pelted with flying books and papers.

"So, you can't see him?" I frowned, letting go of the hope that I wasn't the only crazy person.

He shook his head. "No, but I can still feel him and sense him. It comes with my territory. There's also a ghost in the cafeteria, and I'm pretty sure there's one in the teacher's lounge. So, you can see him? Can you see others or just him? How did you elevate him into a poltergeist?"

I took a deep breath, unsure of how much to tell him. As it was only the second day of school, I didn't know him well. What had he met by his territory? Did he mean just the room or some other realm of knowledge that he occupied? From any angle, it was a weird thing to say.

Perhaps I wasn't the only crazy person here. He was just crazy in a different way.

"Your hesitation says it all. You're a Seer, aren't you?" He folded his arms and studied me like he'd discovered a new species of house cat.

"A see-er?"

"It's spelled like seer, but it's see-er. Instead of someone who can see the future, you're someone who can see into the other world. A Seer. Do you see?" His lips twitched at his own joke, but this was not a time for jokes.

"Is that what you are? Is that even a thing? I think he's making this up." Brandon looked Mr. Tyler up and down.

"Are you making this up?"

"So, you don't even know what you are? That's not good. Don't you have a guide? Someone in your family who can help you with your powers, and warn you of those who might want to use them for evil?"

"If he's one of those evils, you probably shouldn't tell him anything." Brandon shifted closer as if he was going to somehow protect me if Mr. Tyler ended up being evil.

But he had a point. I was young and stupid, but not stupid enough to trust everyone. Mr. Tyler didn't feel evil to me, but that didn't mean much.

"I'm sure I'm none of those. This was all just a big mistake. I'd better get home now. I'll get those notes from Noah, after all. See you in class!" I lifted my hand in a short wave and dashed down the hall.

"Wait—I can help you!" His voice echoed as I jogged away from him. "A Seer shouldn't be alone to figure this stuff out!"

The sound my backpack made as it rhythmically hit my back was the only answer I left him.

Chapter 11

"Well, that got weird."

I glared at Brandon icily as I strode home. After having run all the way out of school and into the parking lot, I was out of breath and panting while I talked. "What did you expect when you met a girl who can talk to ghosts? Everything about my life is weird."

"Can't argue with that. I just meant that it was weirder than normal? Your teacher didn't act like a regular person should when finding out his classroom was haunted. Also, he said a lot of weird things I didn't understand. Seer? Poltergeist? He knows more about you than you know about you." He kept pace with me easily as I walked briskly, but then again, he didn't have actual muscles and lungs that needed to work.

I took several deep breaths, trying to calm my racing heart, my heaving lungs, and my swirling brain. It was early evening and while it was still warm, a soft, cool breeze flowed through the neighborhood. A couple cars drove by us as people returned home from work. A man was mowing his yard while kids played in the grass next door. If anyone stopped to take a good look at me, they'd realize I was muttering to myself, but I almost didn't care at that point.

"If he knows so much, why hasn't he gotten rid of the ghost?"

"Didn't he say something about the ghost not bothering him up until now? How did you make it so mad? Why does it bother you so much?"

"All these questions you keep asking aren't helping me figure anything out. It's obvious that I don't know what I'm doing. I don't know why it's happening to me, but I do know that I hate it." I kicked a weed with my shoe to illustrate my point.

Brandon stepped out in front of me and made a completely normal gesture to place his hands on my shoulders, but of course they went right through. He frowned slightly, but he'd gotten the effect he wanted. I stopped walking and looked him in the eyes. It was odd seeing someone but looking right through them. He was a blue shade all over, and I couldn't tell what color his eyes had been when he'd been alive except that they had been light, perhaps blue or green.

"I know you hate being able to see and hear ghosts." His expression was focused but there was kindness in his eyes. I wasn't used to a ghost showing me kindness. Usually, they just wanted something from me. "And I'm sure it's odd, and you feel alone, although funny enough, you've got like double more people to talk to than the average person, but you feel alone because none of the living can see and hear as you do. I'm sure you wonder if you're crazy all the time."

My eyes broke away from his, and I looked down at the tops of my tennis shoes. Maybe if I didn't look right at him, the tears wouldn't spill out. "If I don't acknowledge the ghosts, then it's like I'm not actually crazy. I can convince myself that they aren't there, and I don't need intensive therapy or some kind of miracle drug."

"Alright. I can understand that, and even though we have lots of questions, I do know some things. First, you are *not* crazy. Well, no crazier than anyone else. Your teacher felt the ghosts. They are really there. You're special. You can see them."

I kept looking at my shoes until Brandon peered down far enough that his face went into my line of vision. I followed it until he stood straight again. He wore a half-smile, and my lips almost copied his.

"Second," he held up two fingers, "there is at least one ghost who is beyond grateful that he has someone to talk to. And while I would have been all right being able to talk to just anyone, you are not just anyone. You are smart and hilarious and more than nice to look at. Your friends are dopes for not seeing how awesome you are."

"They're dopes, eh?"

"Yes. I mean, that one kid might like you, but he's a dope for letting that other girl boss him around so much."

Laughter bubbled up inside of me, and I let it out. A giggle escaped my lips that was sure to earn me looks from bystanders.

"I really need to get some earbuds so when people see me talking to myself, they think I'm on an important phone call."

"I don't know what earbuds are, but sure, that sounds nice." Brandon smiled and I realized, despite the fact that he was a ghost, I was grateful for him, too.

There was no way I would admit that, though. The last thing he needed was more confidence.

"Are you going to follow me all the way home?" I began walking again. Even though I could have passed right through him, I figured the polite thing was to walk around.

He fell into step next to me. "I won't if you don't want me to. I don't want you to be getting sick of me. There's only so much good looks and witty charm a person can handle in a day."

I shook my head. "I'm not sure you could even fit inside my house with that big head of yours."

He shrugged. "Good thing I'm incorporeal or something. I'll pass right through, even with my big head."

I laughed again, feeling it lift my heart, even if just a little. "Alright, you can come with me, but I draw the line at my room. You can stay for our totally uncomfortable family dinner, meet the family, and then when I get to my room to finish my mountain of undone homework, you'll have to go home."

"Fair enough. I hope your family likes me."

"I'm sure they'll feel so comfortable having you around, they won't even realize you're there."

"Funny. So, what are you going to do about that teacher ghost?"

I sighed and felt some of the tension ease out through my lungs. "I have no idea. I mean, I have my list, but what if I try the second thing, and it doesn't work, and he just gets madder?"

"What's the second thing?"

"You'll think it's stupid."

He shrugged. "I might have been a ghost for over twenty years, but that doesn't mean I know anything about it. At this point, we're dealing with the supernatural and abnormal. Everyday ideas and rules aren't going to work here. Why would you be stupid for trying to figure it out?"

"How old are you?" I squinted at him in the evening sunlight. "Surely you're not that much older than I am."

"By years that I was actually coherent and a person? I was two months away from eighteen. By years of when I was actually born... er—" he counted on his fingers for a second, "thirty-nine?"

We both laughed at the idea. Thirty-nine seemed ridiculous.

"I was going to say that you seemed older than that by some of the wise crap you spit out, but definitely not thirty-nine."

"Thank you?"

I grinned. "You're welcome. We should make sure to celebrate your birthday. Eighteen is a big deal."

"I thought you were trying to get rid of me. Maybe once you figure out how to get rid of this teacher ghost, you'll try to help me cross over, or whatever the cool kids are calling it these days." He said the words nonchalantly, but there was a tightness about his mouth that made me think he wasn't keen on the idea.

"Do you want to go? I mean, is there like a bright light beckoning and you've just been ignoring it? Do you think you'll go to heaven? Heck, do you even believe in heaven? What happens when you die, anyway?" The questions spilled out of my mouth, and I felt a little bit mad, like the *Alice in Wonderland* kind of mad. I could have pulled my hair out for emphasis.

"Woah, slow down, friend. Your brain is going to overload and explode. These are some deep questions."

I took a few breaths, trying to calm down.

"Did I see a light? No. I do believe in Heaven, but I'm not sure if I'll go there. We all make mistakes and how strict are heaven's rules? According to the bible, just lying once will get you into Hell."

"By those rules, no one can get to Heaven."

"Exactly. I'd rather be a ghost than go to Hell."

"I suppose that makes sense. So, you want to stick around? You don't want me to banish you and send you where you belong?"

Brandon stopped at a particularly large and blooming bush and took a big whiff. He probably couldn't smell anything but perhaps he was able to remember it. "Being a ghost isn't so bad."

"Alright, fine. I won't send you away until you want to go away, deal?" I stuck out my hand for a shake.

He smiled and put his hand in mine. Neither of us felt the contact, but it was the thought that counts, right?

"Deal."

"Great. So, we're almost home. Later, I need to get a hold of that Rose lady to see if she'll help me banish that ghost. She seemed like she knew what she was talking about. It's clear at this point that I need more answers, and I need help."

"You are clearly lost."

"Thank you."

"Any time."

My neighborhood was built all at the same time in the 80s. The houses weren't new, but they were sturdy and updated enough that the place didn't look rundown. My house had a nice porch and while the siding was dated, we'd put on a new metal roof a few years ago that helped its appearance. It wasn't great, but it wasn't terrible either. Since my parents weren't rich, one being a college professor, and the other a photographer, it was a house that suited us. Would I have liked a bigger and better one? Of course, but I also knew there were people who didn't have a house at all. Perspective is important.

"Here we are. Home sweet home." I gestured vaguely at the house as we walked up the lawn.

"Better than a skatepark."

"Fair."

I tossed my bookbag onto the couch as we got inside. My mom hated that I left it there, but it was a good reminder to do homework instead of bingeing TV. In fact, we nearly had the same conversation every day.

"Can you please put that bag in your room? It doesn't belong on the couch," Mom said by way of greeting from the kitchen.

We had an open floor plan so she could see the whole front room from the kitchen.

I sighed. "It helps me remember to do my homework. You want me to do my homework, right?"

"Can't you set an alarm on your phone or something to help you remember? Why do you even need a reminder, anyway? Don't you have homework every night?" She barraged me with questions while filling up a pot of water.

Grandma stood behind her, eyeing the pot carefully, making sure she was doing it right. I never got the nice Sunday evening dinner at Gran's since she'd died while I was young, but I could tell from the way she interacted with my mom, she had been a meticulous and caring cook. My mom, however, liked to wing it. Her food wasn't terrible, but I'm sure it wasn't the awesome stuff my grandma had been capable of. I knew firsthand how mom's cooking was never on level with Gran's idea of how food should be.

"Yes, I do. That's why I need to make sure I remember. What if I forgot to do it *every night*? That would be terrible!" I hopped up on a barstool. We had an island in the middle of our kitchen with four barstools where we usually ate breakfast. For dinner, we used the table.

Mom shook her head and sighed. "I won't be winning this argument, will I?"

I smiled and pulled out my phone to check for messages. "Nope."

Grandma's preoccupation with my mom's cooking ended abruptly when Brandon walked into the room behind me. He'd been checking out the front room and muttering polite compliments on my mom's knickknack collection of figurines.

"Oh no." Grandma's face was already pale and blue, but it went even paler, if that were possible. "Not the baby."

She rushed over to me and tried to grab my shoulders. This was the first time I'd had such interaction with her, and it was difficult to ignore. I kept my eyes pinned on my phone.

"Please tell me you don't have it! There's only supposed to be one person per generation! Hanna, please tell me you didn't bring a ghost home from school like a lost puppy dog. We *cannot* keep him." Her voice was panicked and pleading.

Mom's back was to me as she pulled noodles from the cupboard and sliced thick bread. "How was the second day of school? Did you see Noah again today?"

Brandon sat on the stool next to me and watched my grandma have a panic attack as she tried to shake me away from my phone. "I think she wants to talk to you. Also, I *am* as cute as a puppy, and just as lost."

I pressed my lips together, bracing myself for the guilt I needed to confront.

"It was fine," I said in reply to my mom's question. "Yes, I saw him."

The second statement was for both Gran and Mom. I looked into Grandma's eyes for the first time as I spoke, so she knew that was meant for her.

I swear she almost fainted.

"Was Andrea hanging all over him still?" Mom glanced at me with a knowing smile and then went back to cooking.

"How long have you been able to see ghosts? Oh, this is not good." Gran stopped grabbing at me and began pacing back and forth.

"Yeah, of course. Andrea loves Noah so much." I made a gagging sound for everyone's enjoyment. "It's gross. I've been watching them for years."

"Yes, you have been friends with them for a while."

Gran paused in her pacing. "Years? Is this the first time you've seen me?"

There it was—the question I had been dreading. How do you tell your grandma you've been avoiding her for thirteen years?

Chapter 12

"Rut ro, raggy," Brandon said in a horrible Scooby-Doo voice.

I shook my head slowly while I looked at Grandma. I hope she could see the guilt and regret in my eyes.

She frowned and continued pacing. "All this time it was your powers helping me be here. Oh, this changes so much. We'll have to get another necklace, but I'm not even sure that's possible. How could there be *two*?"

"Why do you need a necklace? There's someone else who can see ghosts?" Brandon asked the questions I couldn't while Mom was standing a few feet from me, stirring the sauce and humming to herself.

Gran stopped her pacing and peered at Brandon. "Who are you, anyway?"

He sat up straight. I kept looking at my phone, wondering if I should try to take this conversation elsewhere, away from my mom's ears.

"What? Who me?"

Gran walked through the kitchen island to stand next to Brandon. Her eyes narrowed as she looked him up and down. "Is this your boyfriend? You can't date the dead, you know."

I choked on my spit while Brandon chortled heartily.

"Are you alright?" Mom turned around while still holding the sauce spoon. A few drops fell to the floor.

After coughing, I got a hold of myself. "Oh, I'm fine. I'm just going to head to my room for a bit. I'll be back for dinner."

She quirked her eyebrow but nodded, and I left, hoping my new entourage would follow so we could straighten some things out.

"Okay, listen up," I pointed at Brandon after shutting my bedroom door, "you are *not* allowed in here unless I say. This is a onetime deal."

Gran nodded. "No boys in the bedrooms."

Brandon rolled his eyes. "I'm not sure what nefarious plans y'all think I have but fine, I get it. No boys allowed."

"Gran..." I sighed, unsure where to start. "I'm sorry for ignoring you all these years. I was too scared and didn't know what to say."

"Come sit here." She patted the bed next to her and then pointed to the chair by my desk. "The boy sits there."

Brandon complied, probably just happy not to be alone at the skatepark even if he had to deal with a crabby grandma.

"First off, please don't be sorry." She tried to grab my hand that was sitting on my lap. Even though she made no contact, she left it there. My skin was cold, but that was all I could feel. "I'm the one that should be sorry. There is a lot to being a Seer, and you've had no one to help you. I'm sure you've been very confused."

There was that word again. I nodded.

"Confused enough, it seems, to have befriended one and let him follow you around like a lost puppy." She gave Brandon a pointed look.

"I don't mind being a puppy." He grinned.

"We only met yesterday. It's not like he's moved in or anything." I felt defensive, but I wasn't sure why. Hadn't I been thinking the same thing to myself all day? "I just needed his help earlier, and then we got to talking, and then he's here for a bit. He'll go home soon."

She sighed and looked to the ceiling. "Heaven help us. If I had been there for you, you wouldn't need the help of a ghost. Well, besides me as a ghost, funny enough. What kind of help could he offer you, anyway?"

Brandon stuck out a pouty lip. "I can be very helpful, thank you very much... At least, that's what my mommy always said."

Despite my grandma offering to help educate me in the ways of being a Seer, or whatever I was, I was still hesitant to open up to her. It seemed like her methods were a lot different than mine, so far. She might have been able to help me, but was it the help I wanted?

Then again, I'd rather trust her than a teacher or a psychic I didn't really know.

"He was helping me as a lookout. I was trying to cleanse a classroom at school and needed someone to warn me when the teacher was coming back. Turns out, ghosts are useful for that since no one else can see or hear them."

"Oh, right. You wouldn't know. Okay, we'll get back to that later. Yes, that's true. Ghosts can make a good lookout, until they go crazy, that is. One shouldn't rely too much on ghosts. They're unstable." Gran patted through my hand. "I realize I'm a ghost saying this now, but I understand the limitations. Most other ghosts do not."

"What kind of limitations?"

"A ghost needs to be very careful where they place their energy, or they might lose themselves. That's why ghosts can't interact with the material world. I mean, they can, but it takes more energy and where do you think that energy comes from? We can't eat like humans."

I glanced at Brandon, waiting for him to become unstable at any moment. He gave me a cheeky grin.

"I suppose I better tell you about the teacher ghost then."

She nodded, eyes focused and giving me all her attention.

"There's been a ghost in my history class the last two days. I've gotten pretty good at ignoring ghosts—"

"Which I should know all about."

I winced. "Fair. Again, I'm sorry."

She smiled and waved it off. "You have plenty of time to make it up to me."

"But this ghost is so loud and lectures all during my history discussion with the other teacher. It's difficult to pay attention, and I'm worried about looking crazy in front of the other students or getting a bad grade because I can't focus well enough."

"Understandable. I've met a ghost or two like that."

"Which reminds me that I haven't asked how you know so much about ghosts. Were you a Seer too?"

"I was. I am, however you want to look at it. I've got more stories about ghosts than I can say."

"I'd love to hear some, sometime. I'm sorry we didn't get more time to bond while you were alive." I frowned and found that those words were true. I had been robbed from yummy grandma cookies and giggle chats on Sunday evenings. Sure, I had my dad's mom who was still around, but she was more of the traveling type, and we only visited with her once or twice a year. I got the sense that with Grandma Carey, my mom's mom and current ghost, we would have been a lot closer.

"I know, dear. I'm sorry. Death comes to all, whether we're ready for it or not."

"Amen to that," Brandon said, referring to his own death that I still knew nothing about.

"It's okay, Gran. We can bond now, even if you are dead."

She smiled and I was comforted, for some reason, that she still had cute eye wrinkles and smile lines. "Exactly. So, continue your story about that teacher ghost. You were trying to get rid of him this afternoon?"

"Yes. I read that white sage would help cleanse the air, bought a bundle today, and tried using it all over the classroom while Mr. Tyler was getting a copy of notes for me."

"And boy did she make him mad. Books and papers were flying everywhere!" Brandon supplied, not-so-helpfully.

Gran's eyes widened. "Did anyone get hurt?"

"Not yet. We still have class to go to though, and that ghost is still in there. I need to do something else, something stronger, to get him out."

"This might have seemed obvious to you, so I mean no offense when I ask this, but did you try talking to him?" Grandma gave me a look over her ghostly bifocals.

"That's what I said!" Brandon threw his pale arms into the air in triumph.

I put my eyebrows together and frowned. "I haven't talked to you since you've shown up, why would I talk to him?"

She nodded. "Alright. Talking to ghosts can be very overwhelming. I get it. But that's really the only way to help them. You need more information about his life and what happened in order to help him finish his business."

"You mean that's a real thing? I'm supposed to help all ghosts in all the world with their unfinished business just because I can see and talk to them? That doesn't seem fair."

"I know. Oh boy, do I know, but that's just the way of it. You can try looking at it as a gift, rather than an unwanted responsibility."

"Dinner's ready!" Mom called from downstairs, saving me from having to respond to this ludicrous idea.

"Coming!" I yelled to the door and then looked back at Gran. "I'll keep your advice in mind. But first, I need to try this other thing."

"I'm not sure—" Gran started, but I had already jumped off my bed and swung open the bedroom door.

Trina met me in the hallway as she headed towards the kitchen as well. "Oh, hey. Are you actually going to eat anything today?"

Gran and Brandon followed behind me, and Trina was lucky I was too busy thinking about all the crap I had to deal with so I didn't smack her.

Dinner was less dramatic than the day before but still tension-filled. Mom and Dad barely talked to each other, Trina pouted about not being able to use her phone at the table, and I shuffled my food around, worried about gaining weight from the carby noodles.

"You really should eat something, m'dear," Gran said over my shoulder.

I sighed. One of the reasons I hadn't talked to my grandma yet was because I was worried about her haunting me instead of Mom. It looked like I had been right about that assumption. Now that she knew I could hear her, she was going to say everything to me. She better not expect me to repeat her messages to Mom. The last thing I needed was to be thrown into an asylum because I was having daily conversations with my dead grandma.

"Are you alright, Hanna? How was school today?" Mom interrupted the quiet I had stirred with my sigh.

"She's fine. All of my friends wanted to sit with her friends today for some reason. It was weird." Trina took a bite of garlic bread and it crunched between her teeth.

"Really? Are you two starting to hang out together?" Mom's eyes got shiny with hope. All summer she'd been prompting Trina to try and support me at the new school by hanging out with me.

Trina shrugged. "I guess so."

"Why did Caleb want to sit with us? It *was* weird." I looked at Trina, trying not to seem too eager to talk about Caleb.

"I know, right? It doesn't make sense, especially after the angry way that other kid looked at him."

"Noah. Yeah, he looked so mad. I don't get why Caleb would want to face that anger to sit at a stupid table of sophomores." There were a few guesses I had, but I didn't want to voice them. It was embarrassing to assume Caleb had sat with us because he'd wanted to spend more time with me.

"Maybe he has a crush on one of your friends? Isn't that one girl a cheerleader?" Trina swirled noodles around her fork until they were tightly woven.

"Andrea, Randi, and Stephanie all are, actually. The one who was sitting across from me was Andrea and Stephanie was the one Caleb sat by."

"Oh right, the flirty one."

"That's the one."

"There are very few reasons teenage boys do anything," my dad said, proving he'd been listening even though his focus had purely been on eating.

Mom looked at him and nodded sagely, perhaps glad that he was participating in the family discussion. "That's true, girls. And do you know what that is?"

We both rolled our eyes as she launched into her "be careful of boys" speech. Brandon had taken a seat at the island on one of the stools and practically giggled throughout the rest of dinner. Luckily, I had heard the speech many times or else his giggling might have been too distracting. Gran shook her head and kept giving me pointed looks like she was upset with the boys (well, the one dead boy) that I had chosen to hang out with.

Dad left the table first, having finished his dinner quickly without talking much, except for the boy lecture. After rinsing his plate, he started emptying the clean dishes from the dishwasher and putting the dirty ones inside. Mom's eyebrows went up in surprise as clinks and clanks came from the kitchen, but she must have appreciated it because her lips almost loosened into a smile.

After shuffling my pasta around and taking a few bites of the soggy green beans, I felt I'd done enough and excused myself from the table. Gran and Brandon followed me into the hall, and I turned to address them both.

"Alright, I need time to myself now. I understand you guys are lonely, and I'm the only person you can talk to, but I also have a pile of homework and need my personal space. Brandon, I'll make sure to stop by tomorrow and visit you, okay?"

"I would make you promise, but I don't want to sound that desperate." He smiled but there was a tightness around his eyes that made me feel sad.

What was it with this kid, anyway? Ugh, making me feel things.

"And Gran, you can go back to hanging with mom or whatever you want to do, but I want to be clear that my bedroom is a ghost-free zone, okay? I need to have peace in my life and have at least one place I can retreat to, so my thoughts don't bombard me into insanity."

She nodded slowly and as I looked into her eyes, I felt another pang of guilt and sadness.

"I know we've lost time between us, but there is still plenty we can use to bond, okay?" I said, hoping to get rid of some of the guilt before I ended up spending all evening with her and not doing any of my homework.

"I know, sweetie. I'm torn because I'm sorry you've got the burden of this family power, but I'm also selfishly relieved that we can spend more time together, and that I'm not so alone anymore."

"It's alright. We'll get through all this together." I smiled my most encouraging smile and waved to both before going back into the front room and grabbing my bag off the couch.

I was surprised to see Trina leaning against the wall, her arms folded. Her amused eyes told me she'd seen enough, if not all, of my odd conversation.

"Er—I, uh," I stuttered, unable to think of a plausible excuse.

She pressed her lips and considered me for a moment. Then she shook it off and headed towards her own bedroom. "Have fun doing your homework."

I was relieved she hadn't said anything but also felt unnerved. Shouldn't she have been worried about her sister talking to herself?

Chapter 13

I fell asleep that night on my bed in between books, pens, and notebooks. How I had so much homework on just the second day of school was beyond me, but I got most of it done, including the math worksheet Andrea was sure to ask about during lunch. When I awoke in the morning, my neck was stiff, and I had a headache.

As I got ready for school, I worried about history class. Was the ghost still mad? Would we be able to even have class in the same room? If so, would he be more distracting as I tried to focus on Mr. Tyler?

It was clear I needed help to get rid of him, and there was only one person I knew that could help me the way I wanted.

As I walked into the kitchen for breakfast, Gran fazed in through the wall. "Hi, there. Did you have a good evening? Get all that homework done?"

No one was in the kitchen with us, but I still made sure to talk quietly in case they could hear me from other parts of the house. "Most of it. I'm sorry I needed to kick you out for some space."

She waved her ghostly arm. "I understand. If anyone in the whole world understands, it's me."

"It's weird to think that someone else can do the same things I can. It's even weirder to think of it as my grandma doing it." I picked up a banana from the counter and considered how many calories it had.

"I'm sure it is, dear. It took me a while to come to terms with what I could do, but eventually, I felt bad for the ghosts around me, and I wanted to help them. I started out slow, but the best technique I found over the years was always to start with talking to them. You'll be amazed what you can find out if you ask."

I sighed, decided that eating a banana would probably be okay, and popped the peel open. "Talking with ghosts has never been good for me. They flock towards me like seagulls on a hot dog, and it's terrifying."

"You seemed to be talking with that young man last night just fine."

"Brandon is different," I said around a mouthful of banana. "I always make sure we're alone. Well, except for you, yesterday, of course."

She nodded sagely. "Promise me you'll be careful. Ghosts can change. They can't come back to life, but they can become something else, something worse, if they let themselves. Plus, falling in love with someone you can't touch, and no one else can see is setting yourself up for heartbreak. There's not a happy ending here, sweetie."

I finished the banana and tossed the peel into the garbage can. Mom whirled into the kitchen in her usual busy morning routine and saved me from having to directly answer Gran.

There was no way I was falling in love with Brandon, even I knew that would be too weird.

So why did my heart sink at her words?

I left for school again without Trina. It wasn't worth it to wait for her and I enjoyed the early morning walks while sunshine passed through the trees that rustled with the cool breeze. My opinion might change when it got colder, but until then, the walks were soothing and enjoyable.

As I walked through the parking lot towards the side doors of the school, I saw a familiar person standing nearby, leaning on the brick wall and watching me walk. His tan skin shone golden in the sunlight and his white teeth dazzled me from several feet away.

"There she is."

"Hey, Caleb," I said breathlessly. "Were you waiting for Trina? She usually parks on the other side of the school and runs late to class."

"Nah, I was waiting for you." He stood as I approached him. "Can we talk for a second?"

My eyebrows rose so far up my forehead, they were in danger of popping off. "You want to talk to *me*?"

He chuckled, a deep rumbling sound that tickled. "Of course. We're friends now, aren't we?"

"I thought you were Trina's friend?" I felt lame for saying that, but it was the truth, wasn't it?

"Can't I be both?"

"I guess, but she's clearly the cooler of the two of us."

"Are you trying to tell me who I can and can't be friends with?" The question could have been him taking offense but because the grin didn't leave his face, it was probably okay.

"Hey, I was just warning *you* that hanging out with me isn't cool, but it's your social life." I returned the grin.

"I'm sure I'll survive." He grabbed my hand and tugged me towards the outside benches that lined the sidewalk.

His skin was cool to the touch, but heat grew from his contact and traveled up my arm. I was still breathless, but it wasn't from walking quickly. Thoughts spun around in my head as I tried to figure out what was happening. Surely no one this hot and cool could be interested in me, right?

Caleb pulled me down to sit next to him on the bench. The cement was cold through the fabric of my jeans, but I welcomed the chill. Hopefully, it would cool me off.

"What do you want to talk about? If you're interested in knowing more about Trina, you could ask her. Her favorite color is pink, and she loves to hang out on Friday nights with her girlfriends, painting toenails, watching movies, and gossiping. Her favorite—"

He put a hand up to stop me and laughed. "Woah, slow down. We're not here to talk about Trina."

"Oh, okay. Oh! Maybe you can tell me more about Mr. Tyler since you had him as a teacher a few years ago? Did you ever notice anything odd about him?"

A slow smile stretched over his face. "Is his friendly-teacher routine not fooling you?"

"What? No, he seems friendly enough. I'm not sure how to explain this, but like he seems to know things that are different than other people?" I knew I was botching it, trying to get information from Caleb without saying exactly what I was curious about. It was hard to pretend to be normal while trying to get abnormal information. "I was wondering if you'd heard anything weird about him or something. That's all."

Caleb nodded. "Yeah, he's not your normal history teacher and he might need to shave more often than most of us, but overall, with me around, he's harmless."

"Okay..." I wasn't sure what to make of any of that.

"But that's not why I wanted to talk to you. We need to talk about Noah."

I blinked. "Noah? My friend that you barely know from football practice? You two seemed to hate each other. What's up with that?"

"Let's say we're competitive, on the field and off the field."

"We're talking about sports now, right? Not like the dating field."

Caleb shrugged his wide shoulders. "There, too, sometimes. Look, I can't get into details here, but Noah isn't going to be good for you. There's a lot you don't know about him, and you should stay away from him. It won't be good for anyone."

I chewed on my lip as I considered his words. Conflicting emotions whirled around inside of me, and I wasn't sure which one I wanted to win. First, there was pleasure at seeing Caleb care about me enough to try and mark me as his territory by getting Noah out of the way. Also, I was flattered that he thought there was anything between Noah and me. Noah was with Andrea, and it was all but declared by the way they hung onto each other. Third, I was kind of angry. How dare he think so lowly of one of my friends? I had known Noah for over two years. We'd met in middle school in science and had been friends ever since. How could Caleb know more about Noah than I did? As far as I knew, they'd just met over the summer in football camp. Then there was befuddlement. Caleb was Trina's friend. He'd barely met me two days ago. Why would he feel strongly enough to warn me like this? Perhaps because I was Trina's sister.

Was it possible he was doing this because he saw me as a little sister? That seemed to make more sense than him liking me. There was no way.

"Are you trying to tell me who I can be friends with now?" I tried not to glare at him as I echoed his words from earlier, but the sun was bright, and also, I was mad.

He leaned in closer and put a cool hand on my arm. Tingles vibrated from his touch.

"I know it seems weird and kind of douchey to ask this of you. I know you've been friends with him longer than you've known me, but I need to make sure you understand. He's no good, alright? Being with him will only lead to disaster."

"Disaster seems like a strong word. You're right. This is weird." I pulled my arm away.

Caleb sat back on the bench and sighed. "I'm messing all of this up. Please don't get angry. I'm not trying to tell you what to do."

"Except you are." I glanced at my phone. Classes were going to start soon, and I still needed to get to my locker.

"Okay, fine. You've given me no choice. I know what you are."

All of my bodily functions froze. "Excuse me?"

He looked around, his dark eyes checking to make sure no one was within hearing distance. "You're a Seer. I wasn't sure at first, but from what Noah's said, you're having a hard time in history, and we all know there's been a ghost in that room for ages."

I looked around awkwardly, hoping someone would come up and interrupt this absurdity. "I don't know what you're talking about."

A small smile touched his lips. "It's fine. I'd want to keep it a secret, too. You have a rare gift, and you don't want others taking advantage of you. That's fine. Just know that Noah knows and he's exactly what you are trying to avoid."

I stood up, anger winning over feeling flattered at his concern. "You don't even know him, and if he's so bad, why are you two talking about me behind my back? Maybe you're the one I need to avoid."

The first bell rang, echoing around the parking lot as I spun on my heels and left Caleb sitting on the bench. I heard him curse to himself as I left, and I might have felt some smug satisfaction at having not believed any of his silly antics.

I made it in time to get dressed for P.E. by walking quickly to my locker and stuffing my belongings inside of it. Emma and Addy greeted me with the polite smiles of people who are acquainted but not quite friends. We spent the period having light small talk as we stretched and jogged around the gym.

My thoughts weren't with our conversation as my mind zipped around, trying to dissect the other conversation I'd just left. Who did Caleb think he was, anyway? What did any of this have to do with me seeing ghosts? How did he seem so calm about the whole thing?

It was clear there was much more to it, and I had very little information.

I realized as I walked to history class after P.E. was over, the whole exchange had distracted me from thinking about the angry teacher ghost. Not wanting to run into Caleb again, and unsure about what to do with the ghost, I headed to class through a different route.

Thankfully, it seemed Caleb was busy with confusing someone else because I didn't see him on my walk to class. As I rounded the corner to the 40s, I saw Mr. Tyler standing outside his door, greeting the students. There weren't any books or papers flying into the hall or hear any angry teacher ghosts yelling about any crazy students.

As I stepped up to take my turn to enter the classroom, Mr. Tyler stopped me with an upheld hand and gestured for us to step aside.

"Hey," he talked quietly. It was difficult to hear him over the bustle of the hallway. "I'm not sure it's a good idea for you to come to class today."

"Are you telling me to skip your class? That's a very unteacherlike thing to do." I gave him a strange look.

He sighed, took off his glasses, and rubbed his forehead. "I know. I'm sorry. I just don't know what else to do. The ghost finally calmed down, perhaps running out of energy, but if you go in there, you'll light him up like giving him a full battery."

"So where am I supposed to go? I don't want to get in trouble for wandering the hallways. I could transfer to another history class. I can't keep skipping like this. My parents will murder me."

A look of alarm passed over Mr. Tyler's features. "No! You can't transfer out. You're needed in this class!"

I raised my eyebrows at his passion. I knew I was a good student, but we'd only had one class together. How could Mr. Tyler know I was a good student?

"Er—I mean, that would just be giving up. We can't let the ghost win, you know?"

"Riiiiight," I said slowly, unsure of what to say or how to act.

"Can you try the library? I know this is a crappy thing to do, but we need to get rid of the ghost first or else someone might get hurt."

"That's fair." The hallways emptied out around us as everyone went to class. The tardy bell was going to ring any second now. "I actually do have a plan to get rid of it. Can you meet me here later this evening?"

Mr. Tyler glanced back towards his classroom. "Sure. Are you sure you can do that? We don't want a repeat of last night."

"Yup. Got it completely under control."

"Okay. And again, I'm sorry!"

The bell rang as he walked through the door of his classroom, and I heard him greet the students loudly. I turned away, trying not to feel like I was doing something wrong. Instead of going to the library, however, I headed for the first set of doors and left campus. If I had a few minutes of time, I was going to prepare to get rid of the ghost.

I walked quickly back to that psychic's store, hoping not to miss any of third period again. Not wanting to run into Brandon and lose more time or pick up a ghost puppy, I went wide of the skatepark. The fastest route to the store was down the street where the skatepark was, but I kept to the other side, hoping that it was far enough away to avoid grabbing his attention.

It wasn't.

The small hairs on the back of my neck prickled, warning me of an impending ghost.

"Skipping school again? Why are you on this side of the street?" Brandon appeared with a grin and his hands in the giant pockets of his oversized pants.

I sighed and pulled a few strands of hair out of my face that had flown into my eyes thanks to the wind. "I'm kind of in a hurry here. I can't miss third period again."

"What about second? That's right now, isn't it?"

"Mr. Tyler excused me, so I don't give that teacher ghost more energy to throw books at all the other students."

He nodded. "Makes sense. So, where you headed? Back to that weird lady?"

"Yup. She's going to help me get rid of that ghost, once and for all."

"Have you tried talking to him yet? That might be lots cheaper than paying whatever she charges for services like that."

I frowned. He had a point. How much was this going to cost me? Would there be a better way? Transferring classes would have been so much easier, no matter how much Mr. Tyler wanted me in class or how cool of a teacher he seemed. But even if I happened to avoid this one ghost, what would happen if I needed to get rid of another? Perhaps it was time for me to fight back.

"I didn't think of that. I hope it doesn't cost a lot of money."

"Also, why didn't you just call her? You have a cell phone, right? I've seen kids everywhere these days with phones. They're lots smaller than what I used to have."

"I believe it since you're from before dinosaurs. As for calling her, I figured it would be better to talk about this in person rather than over the phone."

"Okay, but I'm sure she's used to getting all kinds of weird phone calls."

I let the conversation drop, hoping he'd get the hint that I wasn't feeling particularly like having company. We walked quickly down the street while the warm sun beat on my back and the soft breeze tugged at my hair. Brandon's spikes didn't move with the wind or with his movements, but I wasn't sure if that was because he'd had too much pomade in or they didn't interact with the real world since he was a ghost and all.

"Wouldn't it be funny if she told you to talk to the ghost first? I'm pretty sure that's what your cool and wise grandma suggested last night as well," Brandon said after the silence had gone on too long for him.

He clearly hadn't gotten the message.

I whirled around to face him, uncaring what others passing by might think. "Listen, like for real, not just pretend to listen. I am doing this my way. Have you endured thirteen years of ghosts robbing you of all peace and sanity? Have you been yelled and screamed at by dead people so loudly that you can't think, let alone hear anything from what other *real* people are saying? Have you been looked at like you were crazy by every single person you know?"

Brandon took a few steps back and threw his hands up in surrender. "Woah, I'm sorry! I wasn't trying to make you mad."

"And if you're so trusting about what my grandma says, guess what she said to me this morning?"

"Uhm, to have a good day?"

"No! She told me I should stop talking to you like we're friends. Being friends with ghosts is dangerous, and you're a ghost, in case you've forgotten."

"Of course I haven't forgotten. Did you just say we were friends?" Hope filled his eyes, and it made me angrier.

"No! That's what I'm trying to say. We are *not* friends! Go away! I don't need a ghost to babysit me all day!"

"Alright! Sheesh. You don't have to yell." He popped out of existence with a frowning pout.

I stomped down the sidewalk fuming, but I didn't get far before he stuck his head out of a nearby bush.

"Just for the record, I wasn't trying to babysit you. I was enjoying your company."

Then he was gone again.

I threw my hands up in frustration. "Ugh!"

Chapter 14

"Hello?" The bell tinkled over my head as I entered the store. It was the same as the day before—messy, cluttered, and stocked full of weird things I didn't want to look at too closely.

"Oh, good morning." Rose popped up from behind the counter where she must have been stocking something. "Where's your friend today?"

"He's at the skatepark. Sometimes I just need a break—" I stopped talking, realizing she had asked me about a ghost.

The confusion must have shown on my face because Rose laughed. "I couldn't clearly see him, but I can feel when there is a presence in the room. I'm a psychic, remember?"

I nodded, not fully trusting myself to open my mouth again.

"I knew you'd be back." She smiled as golden strands from her blonde hair caught the light coming in from the windows. Just like the day before, it was pulled back neatly and piled on top of her head.

"Yeah... guess you really are a psychic. You probably already know that I need to get back in time for my next class, so I don't have a lot of time right now." I focused on the matter at hand and approached the counter she was leaning on with one hand.

"Well, let's get down to it. Did the sage do what you needed it to do?"

I shook my head. "Heck no. If anything, I made things worse. I need a full out, complete and final banishment. Is that something you know how to do? Or if not, do you know someone who does them?"

Rose pressed her lips together in an almost smile. "Wow, things escalated quickly if you're going from burning sage to needing a full banishment."

I had to admit hearing the words outside my head was a bit disarming. Was I really talking about this to another person? Yes, I was. I'd had enough of that teacher ghost.

"It did. So, can you do it?"

"Yes, of course I can do one." She scratched at her neck for a moment. "I'm not sure you can afford it, though. My services are expert and expensive."

Frowning, I fiddled with the strap of my bag, unsure what it was worth to me. "How much are we talking here? It's just one ghost and all you have to do is banish it. I don't even care if you move it to another haunt or something. I can't have him lecturing me in history class while I'm trying to listen to the real teacher."

"Oh, this ghost is at the school? Not the one that is following you around? How many ghosts do you know?" An odd gleam sparked in her eye, and she leaned towards me slightly.

"Ugh, more than I can count, honestly. No, I'm not worried about Brandon right now, that's the one who came with me into the store yesterday. All I need is the teacher ghost banished. He's driving me crazy!"

She laughed—a happy sound that made the hairs on my arms prick up. "His name is Brandon. How delightful!"

"Er—yes. It's very exciting. Look, I've really got to get back to school. How much will you charge for banishing a ghost from my history class? And how soon can you do it?"

Rose tapped her lips with a manicured finger painted in ruby red. "I usually charge about a thousand for one banishment, with guarantees, of course, that the ghost will never bother you again."

"A thousand?!" My eyes bugged out of my head.

She smiled. "But perhaps I can offer you a discount. You are a first-time customer, after all, who perhaps may need my help more than once."

"Maybe I just need to figure out how to do a banishment by myself." I chewed on my lip, thinking about the money I could get. I'd been able to save some from skipping lunch at school, but it wasn't near a thousand dollars.

"Oh, no. Don't try that. It could end up disastrous. I'm assuming you don't want to make it even more mad, especially after angering it with the sage. It sounds like a very powerful spirit, indeed. Oh no, you cannot do this alone. You need my help." She walked around the counter, shaking her head.

She was right, though. I didn't want to do this by myself. If the white sage had made him angry, a botched banishment might make him blow up the whole school. He was the only ghost I'd seen so far that could manipulate material items. This wasn't something I should mess around with.

"He did seem very powerful."

"Alright, it's settled. You hurry back to school, and we'll meet there later tonight so we can get rid of it once and for all. We'll talk price later, okay?"

I nodded slowly, hoping I wasn't getting myself into something I was going to regret later.

"Perfect. Have fun at school!" She waved cheerily as I left the store. The bell tinkled happily when I opened the door.

"See you tonight," I said before stepping out into the mid-morning sunshine.

Trepidation skittered up my spine. Was this worth getting rid of the ghost? What had I gotten myself into? What was I going to owe her?

I made it back to school just in time for the class dismissal bell of second period. I rushed to my locker, exchanged my stuff and made it to third period on time, out of breath, slightly dizzy, and grateful that there wasn't a ghost in my English class.

It was difficult to focus on third and fourth periods. My mind kept going in circles, thinking about the banishment, my fight with Brandon, and the odd conversation with Caleb. It seemed like the world was against me today. It couldn't have possibly all been my fault, right?

Of course not.

Lunch was loud as students laughed and talked with each other. I made a pitstop again before going to the cafeteria, just to gather myself a bit. As I stared in the mirror, I reminded myself that I was a normal teenage girl, going to lunch with her friends, unable to see the ghosts that kept fazing in and out of the bathroom, most of them girls who looked very lost.

It was not my job to save them. They had turned into ghosts through their own actions of having unfinished business, and it wasn't up to me to fix them. And even if it was, there was no way I could help all of them. There were just too many. It was best not to start.

After I grabbed the usual bottle of water, I looked through the sea of tables to find my friends. My vision blurred slightly, and it felt like something was buzzing inside my head. It was difficult to focus on individual faces and voices. It kind of felt like being underwater, inside a big bubble, while the world went on around me, heedless of my otherness.

Movement caught my eye. Willing myself to focus, the image blurred back into solidity, and I saw that Stephanie was waving me over towards the table.

As I sat down beside her, my knees wobbled, and I nearly fell off the bench.

"Are you alright?" she asked while flipping her platinum blonde hair over one shoulder.

Andrea and Noah were sitting side by side instead of across from each other like they usually did. Randi sat on the other side of Andrea while our other friends and acquaintances fanned out from there. It was hard to miss how close Andrea and Noah were sitting. Their arms were in constant contact from shoulder to elbow. If she had scooted any closer, Andrea would have been sitting on Noah's lap.

Noah looked over at me when Stephanie asked her question. Concern tightened his eyebrows, and he shifted slightly away from Andrea, just enough that their arms weren't touching anymore.

"Nah, I'm fine." I pulled out a smile and hoped they couldn't see it waver.

"You do seem kind of pale," Randi pointed out, unhelpfully.

I waved it off.

"She's always that pale, isn't she?" Andrea fiddled with the tab on her can of Coke.

Randi shrugged and went back to eating her ice cream sandwich while Stephanie gave me a sympathetic smile.

"If you're feeling sick, maybe you should see the nurse? Is this why you skipped second period?" Noah asked, his voice unusually soft.

Remembering the words from Caleb this morning and feeling the heat from Andrea's glare, I shrugged off his attention. "It's all good. I feel fine. Andrea, did you get a chance to work on the math homework? I brought my paper so we can compare answers again."

"Oh, right. Let me see it." Andrea held out her hand, and I passed her the paper I'd dug out of my folder.

As she was scribbling down the answers, I let my eyes wander around the loud cafeteria. Usually, the volume of noise didn't bother me, but today it felt oppressive and droning. I accidentally made eye contact with Caleb who was sitting four tables away with my sister and her friends. They probably had decided sitting with sophomores was annoying. He was so tall, it was easy to spot him over the crowd.

He winked at me which brought some of the blood back to my face. I doubted I looked so pale after that. Then his eyes slid to Noah and back to my face. Caleb pressed his lips and shook his head silently, conveying disappointment for the person I chose to keep company with.

I raised my eyebrows in challenge, rolled my eyes, and looked away, determined not to look his way again. Who was he to tell me who to hang out with? If he knew so many terrible things about Noah, why hadn't he just told Trina so she could warn me about him?

Andrea waved the homework in my face to get my attention. "Earth to Hanna. Your answers all look good to me."

"Cool." I took my paper from her and put it back into my folder.

I was probably dumb for letting her copy my homework every day, but I didn't do it without reasons. Everyone brings something of value to their group of friends. Some bring good jokes and laughter while others bring juicy drama and gossip, building full conversations and excitement. It was my job to bring homework help and support. Yes, it got annoying sometimes and I often wondered if that was the only reason Andrea let me hang around, but that's just how it was.

As Stephanie chatted about some boy in her P.E. class, the walls of the cafeteria seemed to loom in on me. I could have sworn they were moving closer, pushing out the air from the room.

"Where are you going?" Noah asked as I stood up.

"Just going to step out for some air before class starts. I'll see you guys later." I flashed a smile that I hoped was reassuring and confident instead of sickly and trembling like it felt.

"That sounds great. I'll come with you." Noah disentangled himself from Andrea's side and stood up as well.

I was too surprised to protest and so was Andrea, it appeared. I felt her glare sear into my back as we threaded through the tables and other students on our way to the doors. Caleb added his glare to hers when we passed by his table, but I ignored him and gave Trina a small wave instead. She made kissy faces and waggled eyebrows at me, and I rolled my eyes in response.

"Are you sure you're feeling okay?" Noah asked as we stepped through the double doors into the warm afternoon sunshine.

I nodded and took a deep breath of the fresh air. We walked towards the flagpole where there was a circle of concrete benches. A few other students had come out to enjoy the autumn afternoon while eating lunch. Noah picked a bench that was spaced away from everyone else.

Ordinarily, I would have been completely nervous and freaked out by being alone with Noah. I wouldn't have known what to say or how to act and probably would have completely embarrassed myself. I would have let him take the lead on conversation and been content with whatever he wanted to talk about. But after the day I'd had, I wasn't feeling so timid and unconfident. Instead, I was feeling dizzy, annoyed, and angry.

"So, what's up with you and Caleb?" I asked immediately after we sat down. We were a few inches apart and not near as close as he and Andrea had been sitting. However, he did angle his knee slightly so it rested against mine in a friendly way.

Brown hair fell into his eyes as he looked at me with surprise. "Caleb? What do you mean?"

I sighed. "I mean, when he came to sit with us yesterday, you guys were exchanging murderous looks, and then this morning he made a point to wait for me before school and warned me to stay away from you."

"What? Ugh." Noah ran fingers through his hair, and I found my own fingers wanting to follow. "That's just a load of B.S. What did he say about me?"

"It was all very vague and cryptic. Basically, you are not what you seem and there are some nasty secrets in your past that I would be terrified to learn about." I laced some of my words with sarcasm for emphasis, indicating I clearly hadn't believed everything he'd said.

"Look, whatever he said about me is untrue. If anything, you should be avoiding him, not me."

"Yes, I get it. You guys don't like each other, but why? I don't like to follow someone's orders without some kind of explanation. Even my mom gets questions when she tells me not to do something."

The side of Noah's mouth quirked in a half-smile, and I even caught a glimpse of his elusive dimple. "Fair enough. I wouldn't want to be bossed around either. It's just... it's complicated. Some things are not for me to say as they aren't my secrets."

"Well, apparently you have several of your own you can talk about. Care to share?"

"Er—I'm not sure where to start."

I shook my head and sighed. "How about with some truth? If you guys hate each other so much, why were you talking about me behind my back? Why did you tell him I've been having trouble in history class? Why is that any of his business?"

"Did he tell you I said all that?" His eyes squinted in embarrassment.

"What do you think?"

"Alright, fine. You want to lay this out, let's do it," he said with sudden decisiveness. "This isn't just some high school, teenage boy drama. I'm a necro apprentice and Caleb is something else. Let's just say not exactly human."

It was my turn to pull my eyebrows up in surprise. "Say what?"

"I can't say much or I'll get banished from my order. I shouldn't have even said that little bit, but I have a feeling you know more about occult phenomena than other people."

My blood quickened through my veins in apprehension. What did he know about me? How could he know about me? How was this football-playing, cheerleading-dating jock something else entirely? How had I judged him so poorly? What should I say or not say? And what the heck was a necro apprentice?

"Uhm... I'm not psychic or something, if that's what you mean."

Awkward social tip from yours truly: try to play dumb as much as you can when you don't know the stakes. What would it cost me to admit my powers to him? Or what if I confirmed Caleb's suspicions? They were competing for something. Could it have been me? My powers? Whatever it was, I was certain it would not be good. There were too many secrets for it to be good.

"Right. You're not psychic. That's not what I meant. Ugh, this is really frustrating." This time he ran both hands through his hair, flattening it as if he was trying to tame something into submission. "I don't know what you know or don't know."

"This conversation is about *your* secrets, remember?"

"But my secrets could get both of us seriously hurt, or worse. I'll say there is more to life than we can see. There are more forces and powers than we encounter in our mundane, human lives. Some of these powers could be really helpful to certain groups of others."

The bell rang, echoing out across the fields and parking lots around the school. I looked back towards the old brick building and was eager to get to class and out of the second confusing conversation of the day.

"You sound like some religious nut." I stood and looped my bag strap around my shoulder. "I've never known you to be religious, though. This is a different side of you."

Noah also stood and studied me with an intensity that made me pause. "We all play our parts well, don't we?"

He turned and walked towards the school, robbing me of my chance to do a dramatic exit, but his words stunned me for several seconds. Was it possible there were more people that knew more about me and what I could do than I did myself?

My secret was unraveling far faster than I'd imagined possible.

Chapter 15

After chemistry, I had French with Randi. We were getting better at understanding our teacher's French greeting and understanding some of her directions. The class went smoothly, and we didn't really talk except near the end while everyone was working on conjugating verbs.

"Andrea was pissed that you guys left lunch together," Randi muttered quietly while others around us also had quiet conversations. Her brown eyes were wide.

"Why? She hasn't gotten a collar on him yet. I didn't realize he was her property." Oops, still feeling sassy.

Randi giggled and her tight, dark curls bounced. "I can't believe you just said that."

I shrugged and tapped my pencil, trying to will the French words into clarity.

"What did you guys talk about, anyway? You two don't usually hang out alone, do you?"

"Are you the one asking the questions or did Andrea give you an assignment?"

"Wow, harsh."

I sighed. "Look, I'm sorry. It's just been a weird day. I shouldn't take it out on you. You haven't done anything wrong."

Randi dug in her bag and brought out a small granola bar. "Here. Eat this. I've noticed you haven't been eating much at lunch lately, and you seem on edge. You might feel better with something in your stomach."

"Thank you." My hand was shaking slightly as I took the bar from her. "I guess it couldn't hurt."

She gave me a sympathetic smile and went back to her work.

I carefully unwrapped the granola bar quietly. It didn't magically cure all my issues, but the words on the paper did seem to become clearer after I ate.

The last class of the day was geometry with Andrea. The conversation with Randi floated through my mind as I waited for Andrea to get to class. I had yet to have any large confrontation with her. Usually, I was an obedient member of her posse and just went along with whatever the group (which meant Andrea) wanted to do.

I'm sure everyone has that friend who seems to direct what the group is doing, or what they like, or how they feel about different things. If you don't know someone like that in your social circle, you might be that someone. I suppose it's possible that there are groups of friends who don't have someone like this, and I hadn't met the right people yet. Either way, it was harder to go along with it all after consciously noticing the situation.

Andrea slid into a chair just as the late bell rang and that was probably why she slid into a desk closest to the door, not because she was trying to avoid me. At least, that's what I told myself.

Mr. Mink started class, and I suffered through forty-five minutes of brain-numbing math.

By the end of class, and the end of school, I felt drained. When the last bell rang, I could have jumped up and tried to catch Andrea before she left, checking to see how mad she was at me. But I didn't feel like it.

She left without paying any attention to me for the entire period. Admittedly, I had mixed feelings, but overall, I wasn't going to lose sleep over it. There were plenty of other things that were going to keep me awake at night.

As I stared inside the darkness of my locker, trying to get my mind to work and figure out what I needed to take home for homework and what I didn't, Trina gently nudged into my shoulder.

"Want a ride home or do you like walking all that way by yourself?"

The fight had ebbed out of me or else I probably would have fired off another sassy comment. "I guess I could use a ride home. I'm not sure I have the energy to walk all that way right now. Don't you usually take one of your friends home or something? Where are they?"

I looked around the chaos of a school hallway at the end of the day, but didn't see anyone waiting for Trina, not even Caleb.

She shrugged. "Nadine said she could take the bus home today. I just wanted to talk with my sister, something wrong with that?"

"What? Why would you want to do that?" Finally figuring out what I needed for homework, I grabbed the books and shut the door.

"I feel like we haven't connected for a while, and it might be nice?" Trina's blue eyes were round and looked almost vulnerable. Perhaps it was a trick from the terrible lighting in the hallway.

"Fine, but if you start trying to give me advice or counseling, I'm out."

"I make no promises." She grinned and looped her arm through mine as we steered our way out of the school.

We made it to the parking lot and into her car without anyone trying to stop us and confront me about weird things and ghosts. She started her Honda and pulled onto the road.

"So, I wanted to check in with you and see how you were settling in at school?" Trina glanced at me for a second and then returned her eyes to the road.

I shrugged, more out of habit than having her see it since she wasn't looking at me. "It's fine, I guess. It's pretty easy to get around classes once you know what you're doing."

She must have noticed the slightly bitter tone in my voice. "Right. Sorry about that. I should have been a better sister to show you around. I was just so excited to start my senior year. You forgive me, right?"

"I suppose." I sighed. "Thank goodness for Caleb who explained it to me but then turned out to be a weirdo."

While the walk to school took me several minutes, the drive was super short. Trina pulled into our neighborhood and raised an eyebrow at my comment. "What do you mean?"

"Oh, he made some comment to me this morning. He tried to get me to stop hanging out with Noah. Can you believe that? I've known Noah for years and Caleb for what? Five minutes?"

"Hmmm..." Trina thought for a moment. "They did seem to be angry at each other yesterday at lunch. I wonder what that's all about. I'm not sure why he would say that to you but like you've been friends with Noah, I've been friends with Caleb throughout all of high school. He's never seemed weird or untrustworthy before."

"I thought at first that it was because they had some kind of football feud or that maybe he feels protective of me since I'm your little sister." I didn't tell her that my initial fantasy was that he actually liked me and was jealous of Noah. Saying that idea out loud felt ridiculous now.

"Maybe." Trina pulled into our driveway, off to the side so our parents could get into the garage when they came home.

"Well, whatever it is, I'm not going to let him boss me around. Noah might be insane for liking Andrea, but he doesn't seem to be bad or anything."

"Well, either way, be careful. You never know about people, even if you think you might know them." Trina used her key to open the door and we stepped inside.

The cool air from the air conditioner felt nice after the warm humidity of the autumn afternoon. It was quiet in the house because our parents weren't home yet. Dad usually got there later in the evenings and Mom's hours fluctuated all the time. Apparently, my grandma didn't need my mom to be there to show up, at least since I'd started talking to her, anyway.

"Welcome home from school," Grandma's ghost greeted us.

I managed to give her a slight smile before I tossed my bag onto the couch.

"I suppose you're right," I replied to Trina's words, thinking about my conversation with Noah at lunch. Before that, I would have staunchly defended his name, and that I knew he had no secrets in his closet. But now? It was clear I didn't know him as well as I thought I did. What kind of secrets was he hiding?

"Hey, uhm, before Mom gets home, can we talk about something?" Trina sat on the edge of our dad's grey armchair.

"Okay?" I sat on the couch next to my bag and couldn't help feeling like I was in trouble or something. "Am I in trouble?"

She smiled, but it was tight at the corners. "No, I just... I just want you to know something."

Grandma sat on the other side of the couch and primly crossed her legs. "Oh, is she saying what I think she's saying?"

"Did you wear one of my shirts and not return it or something?" I tried a joke to ease the tension. It didn't work.

"Listen, I've been noticing you've had some odd behavior lately, and I'm worried about you. I want you to know I'm here if you want to talk, like ever, even at midnight." She picked at the seam in Dad's chair. "I know we aren't the closest of sisters and sometimes we're too busy to spend much time together, but we're still sisters, you know?"

Grandma sighed and sat back. "Guess not."

"I know. What odd behavior are you talking about?" Perhaps she was referring to the night before when she'd caught me talking to Grandma and Brandon. She'd probably thought about it all night and day, trying to figure out what to say to me. What was I going to say to defend myself? Did my sister think I was going crazy?

"Er—I mean, I'm not trying to pick on you or make you feel bad, or anything, okay?"

"Okay?"

"It's just that I've noticed you haven't been eating well. At first, I thought it was only at dinner, and that you'd had a big snack after school and didn't have room for dinner, but then at lunch I noticed you don't eat there, either. I never see you sit for breakfast in the mornings, and I'm worried about you, is all. No judgments. I just care about you." As she spoke, she fiddled with her necklace, the golden eye gleamed from the sunshine coming in from the windows.

Relief bubbled over me like a humming water fountain. "Oh, that. That's it? You're worried about me because I haven't been eating?"

She gave an encouraging nod and smile. "Do you want to talk about it?"

"Uh, not really. Like you said, I've been eating lots of snacks and forgetting to save room at mealtime. No big deal." I stood and grabbed my backpack. "Well, I got lots of homework to do, and I'm going to my room where I can study in peace."

I said the last part for the benefit of my grandma, clearly indicating I didn't want company.

"Oh, alright." Trina's shoulders drooped as she looked down at her hands. "Well, let me know if you need anything."

I felt bad for Trina who probably took my comment that she was intruding on my peace, but it was better than directly addressing my dead Grandma in front of her, right?

Chapter 16

It was difficult to concentrate on homework as I waited for dinner and then the meeting with Rose after that. I kept thinking about all the weird things people had said to me today. Had there been something in the water? People were coming out all over the place trying to give me advice or tell me random cryptic things that did very little to help me with my current problems.

Even though I knew Grandma had lots of information to give me and would probably help clear up confusion about several things, I was afraid she'd find out what I was planning to do that evening and again try to get me to talk to the ghost. It was the same reason I was avoiding Brandon. I had made up my mind about the banishment, and I wasn't going to listen to anything else. Afterwards, when this whole teacher ghost was put behind me, and I'd learned more about how to get rid of the ghosts, I could sit down and have a long talk with Grandma about my powers and how to avoid seeming so crazy in public or having ghosts scream at me to fix all their problems.

At about five-thirty, my mom texted our family's group text that she was working late that day with a photoshoot and that we were on our own for dinner. That was fine with me. I was sick of having tense and uncomfortable family dinners. Also, I could easily avoid Trina so she didn't sit there like a watchdog and make sure I was eating.

Finally, seven o'clock rolled around. I wish I could say I had finished all my homework and even had time to do a little extra studying for upcoming assignments and discussions, but I couldn't. My brain wouldn't function. The day had been too weird, and I could admit that I was nervous for what was coming next.

Dad was shuffling around in the kitchen when I left my room. I wasn't sure what I needed to bring to a ghost banishment and assumed that Rose would take care of everything, so I was just wearing jeans and a t-shirt with my phone in my pocket and a light jacket.

"I should order out for pizza," Dad muttered as I peeked into the kitchen.

"Don't worry about getting some for me. I already ate," I said with a chipper smile. "Is Mom home yet? She might enjoy having hot food waiting for her."

Dad stroked his goatee for a moment. "She probably would. Are you going somewhere?"

Grandma fazed through the wall as we were talking. She put her hands on her hips and assessed me the way only grandmas could—with just the right amount of judgment.

"I'm going to hang out with some friends for a bit. Andrea needs help with her math homework, again." I added some nice details and an eye roll so my lie sounded legit.

"It's a good thing she has you to help her out so much," Dad said as he pulled out his phone, probably looking for his favorite pizza place app. "Make sure you're home by ten, school night curfew and all."

"Of course. See you later!"

He waved distractedly, his eyes still on his phone.

"I hope you aren't off to go do something stupid. Where's that ghost friend of yours?" Grandma asked as she followed me into the front room.

"Of course I'm not, Grandma," I whispered, checking to make sure Dad wasn't paying attention or that Trina wasn't sitting on the couch or something. "I'm going to hang out with real, alive people. Like you said, being friends with a ghost is a bad idea. You shouldn't see much more of him around."

She folded her arms across her chest and stared at me. "I should hope you will be safe and make good choices."

I smiled. "You know, it's kind of nice to have a grandma who worries about me and wants me to be safe."

"Yes, of course I do. Also, can we talk soon? I have so much to tell you about being a Seer and what it means."

"Absolutely! I would love nothing else but to spend more time with you and get more answers about this. I'm sorry I've had so much homework lately and I've been so busy, but can we talk tonight after I get back?"

She nodded with a smile. "I'll put it in my planner."

"Great! See you later!"

I shut the door behind me and headed out into the evening. The sun sent long shadows to stretch over the sidewalk and road as I made my way to school for the second time that day. The neighbors were busy enjoying the evening with their families, or mowing lawns, or pulling weeds. Birds chirped in the trees overhead and dogs barked as I walked by their yards. The walk was altogether entirely too wholesome for the business I was about to participate in. Hopefully, I could get rid of that old man ghost and get back to normal life shortly. It was going to be nice to enjoy Mr. Tyler's class without hearing all about Abraham Lincoln. It would also be nice not to look like a crazy person in front of Noah.

Rose was leaning on her car in the parking lot. As I walked towards her, my nerves jumping around in my stomach, she stood up and greeted me with a smile. "There she is."

"Thanks for doing this, Rose. This ghost is driving me crazy."

Something twinkled in her eyes as she reached into her car and pulled out a knit bag with tassels hanging off the end. "No worries. I've got you. I have to admit, though, you're different from my usual clients."

"Oh, is that good or bad?" I led her towards the side doors, hoping they were open this late. Mr. Tyler knew we were coming so he'd have left a way for us to get in, probably.

"It's neither, really. People are people. You seem much more in tune with the ghosts, and yet you aren't scared of them. It's almost if, and forgive me if I'm overstepping here, that you're used to dealing with them."

What was I supposed to say to that? "Thank you?"

Rose laughed her happy tinkling laugh and her long, beaded earrings waved with the movement. "I just mean it's refreshing. Maybe you and I can become friends?"

"Guess it all depends on what I'm going to owe you after this." I gave her a pointed look as I tugged on the doors. Thankfully, they swung open easily.

Rose waved her hand vaguely. "No need to worry. I'm sure we'll work something out. Now, tell me more about this ghost. What are we dealing with? Low level regular ghost or do we have a poltergeist already?"

"Er... what's the difference?"

"A regular ghost can't do much to the material world. You might catch a glimpse of them in a dark hallway or hear them whisper or cry out, but they aren't able to move things or hurt people. Poltergeists, on the other hand, are like the next level in ghosthood, if you want to look at it like that. They have tapped into their energy, the power that keeps them here, and they use it to interact with the material world. They can move things, and if they're strong enough, even move things to hurt people. However, since they are using their energy, they soon burn up pieces of who they were before death. The more energy they use, the more they turn into wild creatures full of rage and empty of whatever had made them human."

We approached the 40s hallway as she spoke. Our shoes tapped on the linoleum and echoed around the empty school. Light spilled out of Mr. Tyler's classroom as he waited for us to arrive.

"I didn't realize there were different classifications of ghosts," I muttered, feeling like I should have talked more with Grandma before this after all. "I guess there's much about ghosts that I don't know."

"It's okay," Rose said. "I don't mind teaching you. So, what is it?"

"It's a poltergeist, I think. It was a regular ghost, though, until I tried to shoo it away with the sage. I guess that was a stupid idea."

Mr. Tyler stepped out of his classroom at the approach of our voices. "Hello. I was beginning to wonder if you were going to leave me to fight off this guy by myself."

We stopped walking and met him in the hall. I peered around his shoulder, trying to catch a glimpse of the ghost to gauge what kind of mood he was in. "Has he bothered you today?"

"Not yet. It's been quiet. I haven't even felt any cold chills. Who did you bring with you? Have we met before?" Mr. Tyler extended a hand to Rose. "I'm Mr. Tyler, history teacher and haunted resident."

"This is Rose. She's a psychic? Is that what you are?"

Her slim hand met Mr. Tyler's and they shared a handshake. She also flashed him an attractive smile. "No, I don't think we've met before. I have one of those faces that feels familiar to lots of people." She turned to look at me again. "Some call me a psychic. Others call me a medium. I like to think of myself as a spirit guide."

"Ah, I like that, too. You guide spirits to the next life?" Mr. Tyler dropped his hand to his side.

"In a manner of speaking. Are we ready to begin?" Rose took a step past Mr. Tyler and towards the classroom. "Is this the haunt?"

"Indeed, it is." Mr. Tyler gestured for her to go first, and he walked behind her. "I've known about the ghost in my classroom for years. I'd often feel a cool chill or hear snippets of forceful lectures, but since Hanna here has been my student, the presence has magnified exponentially."

I stayed in the hallway as they talked, afraid of what would happen if I walked into the room again.

"She is special like that." Rose looked around the classroom as she put her bag on the nearest desk. "More special than she knows, probably. So, it sounds like the ghost escalated yesterday and spent a lot of energy. He's probably resting now, recovering. Let's prepare for our work, and then we'll try to get him to come to us. Are you coming in, Hanna?"

"I'm not sure I should." I stood at the doorway and looked around the room, waiting to see him appear and start tossing books at us. "He was pretty angry with me yesterday."

"It's alright. I can handle him. My theory is that your proximity will help feed him some energy, and we'll need that soon."

"Me? Why me?" My heart hammered in my chest as I took a step into the room. You'd think I was used to being around ghosts, wouldn't you? Well, not when it came down to the ones that could throw stuff, that was for sure.

"Like I said, you're special." Rose shot me a cheeky grin and waved me inside. Then she opened her bag and pulled out several items.

I took a few more steps inside, but I kept near the door, just in case I had to run back out again.

"Not to make you feel bad or anything, but I think Rose is right. This ghost hasn't had any trouble in years until you showed up in the classroom." Mr. Tyler's smile was kind, but his words didn't make me feel any better.

"Yay me," I muttered sarcastically.

Rose pulled out five candles from her bag and set them down in a circle. I noticed the candles were white and I remembered somewhere in my research that white candles were good for getting rid of spirits. She also pulled out a pink crystal the size of my palm and a small rope that looked like it was made of hair.

"Is that human hair?" I asked, stepping closer to see what she was using. I wanted to get all the information I could about this banishment in case I needed to do another one, hopefully by myself. I didn't want to have to keep calling Rose for help, especially since I had no idea what she was going to charge me each time.

"Yes, but don't worry, I didn't kill anyone for it." Rose grinned.

"I wasn't worried until you said that," I said with wide eyes.

Mr. Tyler's eyebrows rose but he didn't comment.

"It helps bind the spirit to the other place, so he has less chances of coming back." Rose pulled out a long-handled lighter and began lighting the candles.

"They can come back?" I gulped, imagining the teacher ghost popping up in the middle of a big test. That was not something I needed.

Rose shrugged and her long earrings swayed with her movement. "Sometimes. But not to worry, I offer full guarantee of complete banishment. My ghosts don't ever come back."

"Good to know." It looked less and less likely that I would be able to replicate a banishment after watching one. Perhaps Rose would let me take some classes from her?

After all the candles were lit, Rose stood outside the circle, holding the crystal and hair rope. She turned to me with an encouraging smile. "Alright, here's where you can come in handy. Do you think you could get the ghost to stand in the middle of the circle?"

"How do you usually get them to do it?"

"Oh, a nudge here and a push there. It would be so much easier if you could get him inside though, hopefully without him noticing. I'll be chanting, but it doesn't matter at what point he goes into the circle with my chanting. It's short, and I'll keep repeating it until he's banished. Got it?"

"I guess." I glanced at Mr. Tyler who was standing further back, giving us space. He stuck his thumbs up in encouragement.

"Er—Mr. Teacher Ghost? Are you here? It's that annoying student from yesterday. I've come back to be more annoying." I took a few steps between the desks and towards the front of the classroom. When I looked back at Rose, she smiled and waved for me to continue. "I'm sure I'm a very disrespectful student, and that I need to be committed, or something?"

Prickles danced down my neck, and I knew there was an imminent ghost sighting. I backed up again, standing in front of the circle, waiting to see where he would appear.

"This is outside of school hours and very unusual," a gruff voice said as he came striding through the wall with long legs. "What are you doing here?"

I wanted to back up and hide behind Rose, but I forced my feet to keep still, hoping my body would obscure the circle until I could get him inside.

"Is he here?" Rose whispered behind me after watching my body language.

"Excuse me, Mr. Teacher Sir. Do you have a moment to spare to help me?" I said in part to answer Rose's question.

"Great, okay. Try to get him into the circle without causing him to get violent. I'll start chanting," Rose said from behind me.

"I suppose I could help you, but who are you? You don't know my name, and you are wearing pants. Girls do not wear pants in this school. It's unbecoming." The ghost looked me up and down with a sneer on his face.

So much for women's rights.

"Oh," I glanced down at my pants, "I'm sorry. My dress got soiled on my way to school, and this was all I could find."

He shook his head. "The things they let students get away with these days. It's intolerable. In my day, you would have been beaten for such insolence!"

His voice rose in anger as he continued to talk, and I had to remind myself to keep breathing calmly and look out for any errant books he decided to chuck at me.

"Yes, sir. Sorry, sir. I'll be out of your way in no time. I was just wondering if you could help me understand more about Lincoln's assassination."

Rose's steady voice kept repeating the chant, some kind of Latin, and I hoped she wasn't growing impatient with my lack of progress.

"Why are you backing away like that? Are you afraid of me? As you rightly should be. Respect demands a certain amount of fear. What more do you need to know about Lincoln? My lecture was quite thorough on the subject."

It struck me as how grateful I was not to have this guy as my real teacher. Mr. Tyler was a refreshing glass of cold water on a hot day compared to this guy.

"Yes, sir. Your lecture was quite good. I—I was just hoping to get more detail. That's all." I stopped as close to the circle as I could get without falling into it, but the teacher was not following me. He was too used to standing in command at the front of the classroom.

"I do enjoy a student who wants to dive deeper into the moments of history. I'm sure there are plenty of books in the library that would suit your needs—Hold on, who is behind you? What is she doing?"

The hairs on my arm raised to attention as I felt the energy shift.

Mr. Tyler looked around with concerned, wide eyes, as if he could sense the change in energy, and moved behind his desk, ready to take cover at any moment.

Rose's voice kept steady, and it was her calmness that helped ground me, so I didn't run off, screaming like the little girl that I was.

"Don't mind her. She's just reading from a book. She loves to read. Her name is Rose, and she's a really good student, too. Don't worry about her."

My efforts to assuage the situation did not work. What had Rose said about poltergeists? They use up energy, drawing from their memories and identity until they become a burning ball of rage. It definitely seemed like he was more eager to be angry. Then again, he seemed like he'd been angry his whole life, living and dead.

"This is not a student. What are the words she is saying? Have you brought more insanity into my classroom? Wait—you're the girl from the other night." His face turned a scary, deeper blue while his eyes grew so angry, I expected lasers to shoot out of them at any second.

"Wait, no! That's not me!" I really wanted to run away, but I was afraid of leaving Rose to fight this guy alone. Sure, she was the professional and all, but I had a job to do, and I didn't want to let her or Mr. Tyler down. "It's all right. Just calm down."

"How dare you tell me what to do?!" He bellowed more loudly than when he lectured, if that were possible.

Loose papers, pens, pencils, and books whirled around the room in a dangerous tornado. I wasn't sure what would be worse: a book to the head or a million paper cuts.

"Really!?" Mr. Tyler groaned from behind his desk. "I just cleaned this place up!"

Rose kept chanting, and I knew I had to do something. This approach wasn't working. But what could I do?

With a wave of his hand, the ghost flung what had to be the biggest book in the room at me—a history of medieval Europe. I scowled, unwilling to move and let Rose take the hit. Instead, I grabbed at it, and while the impact still hurt my chest, I managed to catch the book.

"Get out of my classroom!" The ghost roared. "You're just a crazy girl trying to bother me! You must respect teachers!"

"No!" I yelled back, surprised to find my voice was firm. The ghost wasn't the only one who could get angry. "You listen to me! You think you are such a good teacher, but you're wrong! You don't respect your students as human beings, especially not girls, and I hate to be the one to break it to you, but you're actually dead. All your horrible lecturing about Lincoln just distracts me from my actual teacher who is actually trying to teach me something useful!"

The school supplies tornado still spun about the room, but the speed wavered and decreased, as if he was listening to me.

I took it as a good sign and kept going.

"Do you really expect students to listen and pay attention to you if you talk the whole time? That's soooo boring! Have you ever tried asking questions? I bet even the girls would be able to answer some of those!"

That was apparently the wrong thing to say.

"How dare you try to tell me how to teach! You are just a child!"

The whirlwind grew, and my eyes widened as two desks joined in the fray. My hair was whipping all over my face, and even Rose's voice wavered as she tried to keep chanting under the difficult circumstances.

I'd had enough.

"Stop it right now and get into this circle!" I screamed and pointed behind me.

Don't ask me why I thought this would work. Since when had ghosts ever done what I wanted them to do?

I ducked as a stapler flew in my direction.

"My poor classroom!" Mr. Tyler hollered out somewhere behind me.

I was about to yell at the ghost again, when I noticed the ghost was getting dragged through his own whirlwind. The books and papers whipped right through him as an invisible force of some kind pulled him towards the circle.

Rose started chanting louder and bolder.

"What's happening?!" the ghost wailed as he slid across the carpet, unable to help himself.

I crawled out of the way and took cover behind one of the over-turned desks. Peeking over the top, I saw the ghost get pulled into the circle. Once all of him was inside, a white light sealed the circle and shone from the ground. Rose smiled as she kept chanting and the crystal glowed in her fingers.

"Help me!" The ghost screamed as pink tendrils, the same color as the quartz, reached out from the crystal in wispy fingers and wrapped themselves around his arms and legs. They grew and spiraled until he was completely covered.

Rose's chanting grew in intensity while the ghost screamed. Finally, the crystal slurped up the tendrils, dragging the ghost with them, and the whirlwind stopped. School supplies paused in mid-air and simultaneously dropped to the ground in a huge clattering heap.

Rose hastily wrapped the hair rope around the crystal and sealed it with white wax from one of the candles.

"Perfect," she said, appraising the crystal and her work.

Mr. Tyler rose out from behind his desk with wide eyes, his glasses askew, and his bushy eyebrows raised far up his forehead. "Is it over?"

I also stood from my crouched position and fixed the desk I had been hiding behind. "That was intense."

"That was a powerful poltergeist, to be sure." Rose knelt and started putting her supplies back into her bag. She wore a triumphant smile that I supposed came from doing a job well done. "I haven't seen many ghosts that powerful. He was able to levitate all those items at once, spin them, and even pick one at a time to throw across the room. Truly marvelous!"

"Marvelous is not how I would phrase it." Mr. Tyler's shoulders slumped as he surveyed the state of his classroom. "This place is wrecked!"

My heart went out to him. "I'll help you clean up. It is my fault, after all. Like you said, he'd been a decent ghost all these years. It's my fault he got so mad and violent."

"Thank you."

We started up-righting desks, gathering papers into piles, and collecting pens off the floor. Mr. Tyler was really going to have a hard time sorting out all the papers and figuring out which ones would go into what piles.

"Rose, I don't know what we would have done without you." I yanked on a pencil that had punctured a hole in the drywall, grateful that it hadn't been my eyeball. "There was no way that I could have done that myself. Are you sure he's gone for good? That didn't look at all how I pictured a banishment to go. Is the crystal some kind of conduit to the next life?"

Rose had finished packing up her bag and was looking around the room, perhaps assessing if she wanted to stay and help us repair the damage. "The ghost will not bother you again, that is for certain. What did you expect a banishment to look like? A demon from Hell arriving and dragging the ghost down with it?"

She laughed so I chuckled with her.

"Yeah, that would be crazy. No, not like that. Just... the pink tendrils seemed a bit off, for some reason. Honestly, I was hoping I'd be able to learn how to do one myself so I could use it when, er—if I see a ghost again. It would be nice to be able to do that instead of having to bother you all the time, but after watching that whole thing, I'm sure it would take a lot to learn."

Rose focused her gaze on me and took a few steps in my direction. "Listen to me, honey. Banishments are nothing to play around with. You must know what you are doing before you attempt one, otherwise terrible things could happen. You do not want to mess around with the other side."

Mr. Tyler groaned as he stood, one hand on his back while the other clutched another stack of haphazard papers. "I'd listen to the expert here, Hanna. It's probably best to leave this kind of stuff to the professionals."

"Oh, I have no intention of messing with it, especially after seeing that whole thing. We were lucky none of us got hurt."

Both Mr. Tyler and Rose nodded.

"But I would really hate to have to keep asking you for your help. I don't have near enough money to pay for one banishment, let alone more."

Rose studied me with a small smile. "Why are you so sure you'll need more banishments?"

I chewed on the inside of my cheek, trying to figure out how to respond to that. "Er—let's just say I have a feeling, okay? I get lucky like that."

She peered at me, and a prickle skittered up my spine.

"I want to make you a promise, right here, right now."

"Okay…"

"I will always be here for you if you need ghosts banished. Please don't worry about the price. We'll figure something out. I wouldn't sleep well at night knowing you're being disturbed by ghosts when I am perfectly able to help you. I promise you this as long as you promise to keep asking me for help, okay?"

I stared into her grey-purple eyes wondering what she knew about me. Did she know what a Seer was? What was she going to ask of me in return?

My instincts warned me to be careful, but I was more worried about dealing with ghosts like the teacher. Odd things had started to happen around me lately, and it would be helpful to have someone powerful and knowledgeable in my corner.

"Alright, I promise," I said with a firm nod.

"Perfect! Well, you know where to find me." She navigated the paper-strewn floor carefully in her stylish wedges as she headed towards the door. Just before she left, she turned to me once again. "Oh, and tell your ghost friend it might not be the best idea to be hanging out around you while we do a banishment. I would hate it if anything happened to him."

"My ghost friend? But he isn't here." I looked around the room, just to be sure he wasn't hiding behind a bookshelf or something. I wouldn't put it past the nosy kid to be following me when I told him not to.

Then again, he had been pretty mad.

Rose raised her eyebrows in surprise. "Oh? I can feel another ghostly presence here. Are you sure he's not here?"

"Pretty sure. Maybe you're feeling the one from the caf—er, a different ghost." I stopped talking because Mr. Tyler was shaking his head at me and making the "kill it" gesture with his hand slicing at his neck.

Rose gave Mr. Tyler an amused glance and shrugged. "Alright, perhaps it's something else. A school this old definitely has more than one ghost hanging around. See you later!"

Her shoes clicked on the tile as she walked down the hall.

"What was that about?" I asked Mr. Tyler as we kept picking up papers. "And why do you have so many papers in here? This room alone is probably responsible for a whole forest of tree murders."

Mr. Tyler grunted. "Most of it is handouts I use to supplement the textbook. Not all textbooks have all the stuff I want to teach. But I have to agree, after all this, I'll consider going digital more often."

"Why didn't you want me to tell her about that other ghost?"

"Hmmm? Oh, no reason." He turned his back to me as he shuffled papers on his desk, making room for more piles.

He sure had seemed pretty adamant about me not saying anything for it to be for no reason, but I didn't push it. Poor Mr. Tyler had had enough of the paranormal for one day. In fact, I was proud of him for how he had handled it.

Chapter 17

I didn't leave the school until almost ten o'clock. It was probably not a good idea to be alone with a teacher, specifically a male teacher, after school hours, but I had felt too guilty leaving him alone with all that mess. After we'd picked up everything off the floor and straightened the desks again, I left him to figure out what papers he needed for the next day and what papers he could avoid sorting for the night.

The air was chilly, and there was a sharp fall wind that grazed my arms occasionally. I regretted not grabbing a thicker jacket, but I wasn't ready to go home quite yet. Guilt still bubbled inside of me even though I had helped Mr. Tyler.

There was something else I needed to do.

Walking in the opposite direction of my house, I headed towards the skatepark, trying to think about what I was going to say.

How does one apologize to a ghost?

Rose had called him my friend. Perhaps that was exactly what he was, even if he was a ghost. Perhaps that was how I should treat him instead of acting like he was some terrible creature from beyond the grave.

The park was quiet. Streetlights cast odd-colored orange circles on the grass and pavement, but it was dark enough that skating would have been dangerous. Plus, it was too cold for all that nonsense.

I rubbed my arms with my hands, hoping the friction would warm me up as I looked around the park, searching for any movement.

"Brandon? Are you here?"

The rustle of the wind was the only thing to answer me.

I didn't want to go inside the dark park. Who knew what was waiting there to gobble me up? Honestly, I just wanted to run home and snuggle into a warm blanket and drink a steaming cup of tea, but I had to at least try to apologize to him. I hadn't been very nice, and for some reason, I found myself valuing his friendship, despite what I'd told my grandma earlier.

I took a few steps past the fence and into the park, but I made sure to stay within the glowing circle of an overhead streetlamp.

"Brandon, I'm sure you can hear me. Where else would you be? You're stuck in this haunt. Unless you've crossed over? Perhaps your unfinished business was making me say things I regret and now you're in heaven, sitting on fluffy clouds and strumming a harp."

The image of him in his 90s clothes with giant white wings flapping behind him as he played a harp on the clouds made me giggle.

He still didn't answer.

"Listen. I came to apologize. What I said was wrong and rude. I know you're not trying to babysit me. I know you were only trying to help. I shouldn't have acted the way I did."

Still nothing.

"I don't blame you for being mad at me, but I hope you can forgive me, someday." Sighing, I turned around and went back to the safety of the sidewalk.

"Did you get rid of that ghost?" Brandon's voice was quiet as he popped up right next to me.

My heart jumped at his sudden appearance, but I kept from wincing and told myself to quit being silly. I had asked him to appear and should have expected his presence at any second, neck prickles or no.

Something in his gaze told me to be careful. His eyes bore into mine with intensity, almost daring me to be mean or angry.

"Oh, hey. Did you hear me? I said I'm sorry for being so rude earlier." I tried to give him a soft, reassuring smile.

"I heard you."

"Okay, right." The wind moved through us, bringing me more shivers and an awkward silence. "Yes, well, I'm sorry. It's late, though, so I better get home."

"Did. You. Get. Rid. Of. That. Ghost?"

Frowning, I furrowed my eyebrows. "Yes, we did. Rose helped me, and in the middle of a terrifying whirlwind of school supplies, we were able to get him into the circle and banish him for good. Why? Why are you so concerned about it?"

"Why do you even care?" His glare was so icy, I wouldn't have been surprised if icicles formed on his eyebrows. "I've gotten your message, alright? You hate ghosts. You don't want us around and you definitely don't want to talk to us or be friends with one. Why are you here? Why do you need to apologize to a creature like me? Why do you even care what I think?"

His questions were so full of pain and accuracy that it took me several seconds to respond. All I could do was blink, shocked and ashamed of my behavior.

"I can see that you're trying to come up with lies to help me feel better. Don't waste your time." He waved his transparent blue hand vaguely in my direction. "Just be on your way. Do me a favor, though."

I found my voice, but it was timid and cracked. "What is it?"

"Give me a heads up if you're going to come and banish me, too. I'd like to be able to say goodbyes to all my other ghostly friends."

With that last comment, he puffed out of existence and left me standing in the chilly breeze with my mouth open, gaping like a fish.

I didn't bother to try and apologize again. Instead, I spun on my heel and ran down the sidewalk, hot tears sliding down my cheeks.

How could he have thought that of me? I only banished the teacher ghost because he was making my schooling impossible. Grades were important. Getting into a good college was important. Surely Brandon could agree with those facts. Just because I banished one ghost, didn't mean I was out to banish all of them. That would be too much work—I'd never finish.

My thoughts whirled around like the school supplies tornado from earlier. I kept cycling through all the conversations I'd had with Brandon and how he'd gotten the message that I would banish him, too.

It was clear that I hadn't been the nicest to him. I knew that, but he couldn't blame me for struggling to get used to being friendly with a ghost. He just couldn't. It wasn't fair.

By the time I made it back to my house, my nose was running from crying and the cold. Gran had been right. Being friends with a ghost was a bad idea, all around. What could I expect to come of it?

Nothing good, that was for sure.

So, if Gran had been right about that, what else was she right about?

The house was quiet and dark as I walked inside the front door. I could hear mutterings from the TV room while lights flashed from the screen, making the light dance off the walls in reflection. Trina's door was closed as I walked by, but I could see the light was still on, shining through the crack above the floor. She rarely went to bed early.

"I'm home." I knocked on my parent's bedroom door as was their requirement each time we came home from being out at night. It was their way of not having to stay up waiting for us to come home for curfew while still holding us accountable.

"Okay, thank you. Goodnight." My mom's groggy voice sounded muffled from the other side of the door.

Gran fazed through the wall and walked next to me as I headed towards my room. "Out late for a school night, don't you think?"

I sniffed again, hoping to keep the snot from running down my face and made sure to keep my voice quiet. "Yeah, it's super late, but I'm actually glad to see you."

She smiled although her eyes held some surprise. "You are?"

"Do you think you could help me learn more about being a Seer? We won't stay up too late tonight, but maybe you could just start with the basics?"

Chapter 18

It was difficult to get up the next morning. My mind refused to shake off the fog of sleep, and I felt like a zombie stumbling around to get ready. I was so slow that I even managed to finish getting ready at the same time as Trina, and she drove me to school.

I know, right? I was *that* slow.

P.E. helped wake me up as Coach Reed had us run laps around the gym again. Emma and Addison were polite and hung back with my slow jog. They asked me a few questions here and there, but I wasn't very chatty. They must have realized I was in an odd mood because they soon left me to my thoughts.

Gran had stayed up with me for another hour after I'd gotten home. She'd laid out the basics of what being a Seer was all about, as far as she knew it. She'd been trained by her grandma and then had her own life experiences, but that was all she knew about the subject. It seemed there were deeper and weirder things about being a Seer that Gran didn't know about, judging from the odd things I'd experienced only the last few days that Gran had never heard of happening before.

Like why the teacher ghost had been unable to fight me once I'd commanded him to enter the circle.

Or the fact that Brandon could leave his haunt as long as he was with me.

I couldn't even be a normal Seer, let alone a normal teenager. Awesome.

After I'd told her about the banishment with Rose, Gran had seemed surprised about Rose's methods. She remarked how she'd never seen a banishment such as that, but then she shrugged it off, saying how mostly she'd talked to the ghosts, helped them complete their unfinished business, if she could, and watched as they'd gone to the next step, whatever that was.

That's right. Again, with the talking to the ghosts thing—the one thing I just really didn't want to do.

Then she had pointed out how the teacher ghost had had to listen to me and perhaps having to talk to the ghosts wouldn't be so bad. At any rate, it would be more helpful to the ghosts than forcing them to be banished.

I wasn't convinced, but I let the thought float around in my head for consideration. I had to admit that after having met Brandon, it did seem less scary to talk to them, and that for at least one particular ghost, I found myself wishing I could talk to him more.

By the time I got to history class, I was mostly awake and feeling less conflicted. Instead, I felt guilty and ashamed, not a great trade-off. Being sleepy and conflicted was better.

I'd managed to get to class without snagging Caleb's eye. He'd been chatting with some cheerleaders on the other side of the cafeteria as I walked through, and I made sure to walk behind some rowdy boys so he wouldn't see me.

Mr. Tyler was again standing outside his classroom and greeting the students as they walked in.

"Miss North, was it?"

Bree nodded a shy smile as she crossed into the room.

"Excellent. Ah, Miss Sanchez. You look bright and cheery today." Mr. Tyler's smile, half-hidden under his greying goatee, was teasing. "Did you have a late night?"

I scoffed. "You're one to talk, Mr. Under-Eye-Bags."

"Old age will do that to you. At least this morning has been positively peaceful." He winked so I knew he was talking about the lack of ghostly activity.

"Better be," I muttered as I headed towards an empty seat in the back.

Noah came in and sat next to me a few seconds later, offering me a hopeful smile. "Hey."

"Hi." I shifted my notebook to give my hands something to do.

"How are you?" Noah pulled out a pen and notebook from his Nike athletic bag and turned his full attention to me. His hazel eyes were bright from the morning sunlight streaming in through the windows and streaks of gold seemed to shimmer in his hair.

"I'm fine. Er—how are you?"

Right, so I wasn't usually super comfortable when it was just the two of us without our other friends nearby, but after our conversation from the day before (had it only been a day?), I was feeling even more awkward.

How did one navigate such social situations? We all know that I'm not the one to answer that question.

"Mostly just worried about you. I want to make sure that we're good, you know? After yesterday?"

"Uhmm—"

I was saved from answering by the bell, and Mr. Tyler walking up the aisle, starting class.

"Good morning, everyone. I hope you're all bright-eyed and bushy-tailed ready to get into some amazing history."

Noah gave me another hopeful smile and it melted my heart some. He was still that cute friend I'd known for almost two years. We'd never gotten close, mostly thanks to Andrea, but he was a good guy. He worked hard in classes and sports. He was always the first one to mention getting back home for curfew when we all hung out at night. Perhaps he was a bit clueless, and in some weird necromantic order thingy or something, but we all had our own quirks, right?

I made a mental note to ask Gran about it later.

Mr. Tyler pulled the class into a discussion, semi-lecture, and the period passed quickly and peacefully. No ghost popped up and started yelling or chucking books at my head. I was able to answer questions without being constantly distracted, and I have to say the reprieve was quite nice.

Noah turned to me as the bell rang and class ended. "Hey, I think we really need to talk. Can I text you later?"

I smiled like the silly, crush-sick girl I was. Apparently being part of a secret, dark organization didn't stop me from having a crush on someone. Who was I to judge? I was the girl who saw ghosts. "That would be nice."

The next two classes went smoothly. I was finally feeling almost like a regular student. I could focus on my work and was thinking less about ghosts and more about boys—er, I mean, schoolwork.

After my routine stop in the bathroom, I walked into the cafeteria. Smells of school-issue pizza wafted towards me, and I was so hungry, that it almost smelled good. Automatically, my eyes scanned the rows of tables until I found my group of friends.

I had spent the last two classes trying to figure out how to make lunchtime with Noah less awkward. It helped that our friends were there to offer more distractions, but I was still worried it would be weird.

I shouldn't have worried.

Despite what Noah had said to me in the last twenty-four hours and how he'd promised to text me, there he was with Andrea so close to him she was practically in his lap. They were laughing and joking with our friends and as I watched, Andrea giggled, placed a lingering kiss on his cheek, and leaned her head on his shoulder.

Puffing out a breath of frustrated air and deciding that I didn't feel like watching any more of that nonsense, I spun around and headed towards the library. I'd never been to the high school's library, but I'd passed it a few times on my trek through the halls, trying to find my classes. During middle school, sometimes I would hide in the library, but that was before I'd gotten into Andrea's group of friends. The yearning for some peace and quiet rose up inside of me after watching my friend and my crush practically making out in public.

As I was leaving the thundering cafeteria into the relatively quiet hallway, I bumped into a tall, solid person.

"Oh, I'm sor—Oh, it's you."

Caleb chuckled, the sound coming from deep inside his chest. "Good day to you, too."

"Uh, hey, sorry. Was just going to the library. See you later!"

"Wait a second." Caleb grabbed my arm gently and spun me around to face him again. "Why aren't you with your friends?"

"Why aren't you?" I bobbed my head in a sassy way.

He grinned that bright, mega-watt grin that lit up the room. "No need to get grumpy with me. I'm only checking to make sure you're alright. Have you thought more about what I said yesterday?"

"Look, no offense, but take offense if you want. I barely know you. You're my sister's friend, but we've never hung out or anything. Why are you taking interest in me suddenly? Why do you care who I hang out with?"

Caleb's dark eyes studied me for a moment, probably as he tried to come up with some story that I wouldn't hate. "It's like you said: I'm your sister's friend. I got to look out for you, you know, like family?"

I pulled my arm free of his grasp. "We're not family. I barely know you. I've known Noah for *a lot* longer than I've known you. Why should I listen to you? Noah's been nothing but nice to me."

Caleb glanced back into the cafeteria where Noah and Andrea were snuggling like a couple of sea otters and then back to me with a knowing look. "Right."

Scoffing, I turned away. "Go find someone else to bug."

He didn't try to stop me as I left but I heard him speak, his voice traveling easily over the few feet down the hallway. "Come find me when he starts being weird. Then you'll see what I mean."

As I walked briskly away towards the double doors of the library, I made a face and mocked his words in a whisper. "'Then you'll see what I mean'. He's the one being weird!"

The quiet of the library and the smell of books offered a calming oasis from the chaos of the school. I took a deep breath as the doors closed behind me. A few kids who were seated at a table looked up at my entrance, but I didn't recognize any of them. Trying to walk quietly and not disturb the peace of the place, I worked my way past tables, shelves, and computer desks towards the back of the library.

Settling into a chair I'd found in the back corner, I dropped my bag on the floor and my head onto the table. I closed my eyes for a moment and breathed.

While seeing ghosts was my main power, I could detect their presence in other ways. Usually, it was the prickles on the back of my neck that stood at attention, announcing that a ghost was around. Perhaps I was getting stronger at detecting ghosts, probably because I had started spending more time with them between my grandma and Brandon, but even before the neck prickles, something in my mind alerted me that a ghost was nearby.

The new sensation was unnerving, but I did my best to ignore it. I didn't even bother to open my eyes.

A quiet *thunk* on the desk startled me into sitting up and looking around.

"You're going to need to know about these, dear," an aged and kindly voice said as a ghost formed next to me.

She was the same blue, transparent color of all the ghosts I saw. Her hair was styled fluffy, like 80s fluffy, and flowed down her shoulders. She wore a conservative dress with lace ruffles and uncomfort-able-looking dress shoes.

In front of me was a book she had just dropped off. The title was *Phantom Curses* with a picture of a cross on the front.

The librarian ghost smiled at me kindly and walked away, disappearing a few feet down the hallway.

Chills skittered up my arms all the way to my shoulders. Yes, the ghost had looked the same as the others, but she had behaved like none I'd ever seen. Firstly, she had noticed me before I'd even seen her.

Second, she'd used some of her energy to transport a book and place it on my desk. The only ghost that I'd seen move objects was the teacher ghost we'd just banished. Rose had told me using energy like that would make ghosts turn into raging poltergeists, losing their identity of who they were before death until there was only anger left. The librarian ghost hadn't seemed angry at all.

Third, she hadn't wanted a single thing from me. She hadn't asked me one question or demanded that I help her find her lost cat or whatever. Instead, she'd given me a gift and acted like she somehow knew I needed the information for future events. How could she know? Was it possible ghosts could move through time, aware of the future, as well as space?

I clutched my head, worried it would explode from a two-second-long encounter with a ghost. What was happening to me? All of this stuff was spiraling into weirder and weirder events, just because I'd started talking to one ghost kid who happened to like skateboarding.

I should have stuck to my rules: talking to ghosts was a bad, bad idea.

Chapter 19

By the time the last period rolled around, I was exhausted. I was in no mood to handle geometry, let alone try to play nice with Andrea. When I got to class, I sat in a chair near the front, away from where we usually sat, and surrounded by other students so Andrea couldn't sit next to me.

The other students gave me weird looks since I'd chosen a seat close to theirs for the first time. We didn't have assigned seats, but once class had held a couple sessions, people tended to sit in the same spot.

As usual, Andrea made it to class as the bell rang. I tried not to stare at her, but I could see her hesitate out of the corner of my eye. She glanced around the room, saw me, paused as if thinking about what to do, and then slid into her regular chair. My perspective without looking right at her wasn't good enough to see the expression on her face, but I didn't feel like caring at the moment.

Class went smoothly and as the last bell of the day rang, I felt the relief of school being out, my favorite time of the day.

I took my time gathering my stuff up, hoping to avoid Andrea. It didn't work.

"Why are you avoiding me?" Andrea looked down at me while I was still sitting, putting my notebook away.

I tried not to sigh too loudly. "I'm not avoiding you. I'm just really tired today and needed some quiet time."

"You weren't at lunch, either."

She was expert at making a small statement sound like a grievous accusation.

"So? I'm surprised you even noticed." I stood and slung my bag over my shoulder. She was slightly taller than I was, but I didn't feel intimidated by her presence as I usually did.

Perhaps I was growing as a person, who knew?

"I noticed because I didn't have to correct your math homework. You might get lower grades without me helping you."

I rolled my eyes, something I wouldn't have dared to do the day before. "Right. Because you're *so* helpful."

I started to head towards the exit of the classroom, but Andrea stepped in my way. I stared her right in the eyes, and she looked as surprised by my behavior as I felt.

"Listen, no one forces you to hang out with us. You can sit with your sister and her friends or even by yourself, whatever you want. Just don't go acting like we owe you any favors for being your friends. I don't see a line of people waiting to jump into our spot." Andrea's haughty blue eyes darted behind me as if looking for other people who wanted to be my friend.

I laughed and walked around her to leave the classroom. I didn't want her to think that her words had hurt me, so laughing seemed like the right thing to do. I knew if I stood there and tried to come up with a witty comeback, I'd just end up looking dumb.

Tears gathered in my eyes, threatening to do the worst thing ever and spill over onto my cheeks in the middle of a bustling high school hallway. I blinked rapidly, hoping they'd go away somehow on their own.

My hands shook as I turned the dial on my locker. I would have run out the nearest doorway and headed straight home without stopping by my locker if I didn't need some books for homework that night. Despite hours of doing work, I was still behind in my English reading.

I couldn't tell if I upset at Andrea's words, the fact that she had been making out with Noah at lunch, or exhaustion. Perhaps it was everything all at once. Whatever it was, I knew I couldn't keep up with it much longer without having a complete panic attack.

As I pulled out the book I'd gotten from the weird librarian ghost, I paused to look more closely at the cover and the blurb on the back. It was an unusual book that I'd never seen before. In fact, it didn't have any stickers or barcodes to signify it was a library book. I hadn't even bothered trying to check it out because there was no place for the librarian to scan it. Wherever the ghost had gotten this book, it hadn't been our school library.

From what I could tell with a cursory glance inside, it was a book about curses from various sources. There were sections on witches, warlocks, voodoo priests, demons, and even ghosts. I couldn't see why I needed this book, but I wasn't about to throw away free help. Who knew what would happen in the future? Apparently, the librarian ghost did, but I didn't know how to investigate why.

After grabbing my stuff, I left school property. Trina had been standing outside next to the flagpole with her friends, including Caleb, so I hadn't stopped to say hello or try to get a ride home from her.

Perhaps a walk would do me good and clear my head.

Clouds speckled the sky while a brisk breeze flowed through the neighborhood. Autumn was coming and even though the sun was warm on my back, the cool wind reminded me it wasn't going to stay warm for long.

Tears seeped over the edges of my eyes, and I let them trickle since I was alone, and they wanted to get out. It was stupid to cry over a boy, especially one who'd made no promises to me, but I couldn't help feeling sorry for myself.

I must not have looked great because when I got home, my mom took one glance and swooped me into a hug.

"Oh, honey. Are you okay? What happened?"

I let her hug me, taking a minute to breathe in her familiar and comforting vanilla scent. Sometimes you just needed a good hug from your mom, you know?

"Nothing. I'm fine. Just feeling a little down today, that's all." My voice was muffled inside her soft, brown hair.

She gave me another squeeze before letting go. "Your first week of high school has been pretty stressful, huh?"

"You could say that, and there's one more day left in the week. Yippee."

She frowned and tucked a strand of my hair behind my ear, something she had always done since I could remember.

"You really don't look well. Perhaps you need to stay home tomorrow?"

I shrugged. "There's only one day left in the week, and it's my first week of school. I should probably try to go. Why aren't you at work?"

"I didn't have any clients booked today, so I spent all day working on my new website. Do you want to see it?" Her expression lit up in eagerness and hope.

"Sure. Let me put my stuff away, and I'll come see it."

"Great!"

We all know that I usually flung my backpack onto the couch and went about my business, but I wanted an excuse to go to my room, take a few breaths, and clean up some in the bathroom.

Gran's ghost followed me but hesitated at the entrance to my room. I waved her in and shut the door behind us.

"Did something happen at school? Why were you crying?" Gran asked me, echoing my mom. Even though we'd spent very little time together, it was like she already knew me better than my own mom did—Gran hadn't believed the half-answers I'd given my mom already.

"I think it's just stress. A lot has happened the last few days and I feel drained." I plopped my book bag onto my desk and flopped onto my bed. "Have you ever had a ghost notice you before you notice it? Or tell the future?"

"Tell the future? Notice you first? No, never." She shook her head with wide eyes. "What is happening? These ghosts keep breaking all the rules."

"Just my luck."

She sat next to me on the bed, but it didn't dip with her weight because of course she didn't have any. "Tell me what happened."

As I told her the story of the librarian ghost, I rummaged in my bag until I found the book she'd dropped. Gran couldn't hold it in her own hands without spending some precious energy, so I laid it on the bed and let her examine it closely, opening it when she instructed. Together we flipped through the pages, stopping at various odd pictures of witches or items needed to make or break a curse.

"Have you ever seen a book like this before? Did you run into any curses you had to break?"

Gran shook her head again. "No, this is all new stuff to me. I helped ghosts for over thirty years, and I've never seen the stuff you've seen in the first week of accepting your powers. I can't even imagine the things you'll see in your lifetime of helping ghosts."

I groaned and flopped back onto the bed, making the book jump with the impact. "Great."

Gran attempted to pat my knee, but her hand went right through it. "It's okay. We'll work things out together. As you can see, I'm not going anywhere any time soon."

"Hanna, are you coming?" Mom's voice called down the hallway and through my door.

I sighed. "I better go check out her new site."

"She has worked very hard on it all day."

Groaning with the effort, I stood and went to the door.

"You know, food helps restore energy just as importantly as sleep does." Gran looked at me intently over her ghostly spectacles.

"I've eaten plenty," I said and went down the hall and into the dining room where Mom had her laptop set up.

I spent the rest of that evening helping Mom tweak some things on her photography site and get it ready to share with friends and family. She'd been working as an assistant for another photographer, and she'd decided to branch out on her own to see if she could make some extra money.

After that, I holed up in my room catching up on homework. Gran left me alone for a time, choosing to stay in the dining room while my mom kept working, leaving my dad to scrounge around for leftovers. I was glad she was busy because it gave me an acceptable excuse to avoid the whole food scene.

At about ten p.m. I got a text message from a new number.

Hanna? This is Rose. How are you doing?

I put down my English book and read the text message three times before responding.

Hi, Rose. I'm fine. How did you get my number?

Give us psychics a little credit, will ya?

Alright. Cool powers. Are you texting me because you figured out what I can do to repay you?

I like how you get right to the point of things. Yes, can you come by tonight? Are you free?

Tonight? It's so late. What will I tell my mom?

Is there a way to leave the house without telling her?

You want me to sneak out of my house? On a school night? That's not being a very good influence.

Look, I could really use your help. I've got a difficult ghost, and I know you'd be a great help. I could take off some of the money you owe me for yesterday. Just leave them a note in case they go looking for you. You wouldn't want to make them worry, would you?

I paused for a moment and thought about it. I'd never snuck out of my house before, but Gran had said that it was my whole purpose in life to help these ghosts get back to where they needed to. Also, I didn't like having to owe Rose—it hung over my head like a gloomy cloud.

Okay, I'll come. Text me the address.

After changing back out of my pajamas into a t-shirt and jeans, I tucked my phone and a few bucks in cash into my back pocket. I grabbed a jacket on my way out and walked to my parent's door. I knocked politely.

"Yes?" My dad's voice came from the other side.

"Just wanted to let you guys know I was going to bed. I'm not feeling great, and I might not be up for school tomorrow." I kept my voice loud enough to make it through the door.

"Do you need me to come check your temperature?" Mom asked.

"Oh no!" The last thing I needed was her to see me in jeans and a jacket, ready to go out into the chilly night autumn air. "There's no fever. It's okay. Goodnight!"

"Ok, let me know if you need anything. Goodnight."

I walked normally to my bedroom and shut the door while still standing outside, pretending I'd just gone inside. Instead, I tip-toed down the rest of the hall, grateful that Trina pretty much always had her door shut while blaring music and that Gran hadn't come out to investigate. I left out the back door since it squeaked less than the front door and was further away from my parents' room.

I'd had a lot of firsts this week, including sneaking out of my house for the first time. Most girls did that to see boys or hang with their friends. I was sneaking out to rid the world of one more intruding ghost. Was I a superhero yet?

Chapter 20

Thankfully, the address Rose had texted was within walking distance. I was going to turn sixteen in November, and it would be so nice to get a car of my own, even if I didn't know how I was going to pay for it, yet. On the way there in the dark, cool air passing through the quiet streets, I mused at the thought of getting a spunky sidekick friend with cool one-liners and a nice ride.

Too bad I didn't know anyone like that.

When I arrived at the address indicated, I had to double check my map app. It did not look like a place the elegant Rose would hang out at. I noticed her car parked across the street though, so I must have been at the right house. The neighborhood itself looked older—the trees were larger, the houses more run down and in older styles. Some of the houses had been kept up, but the one I stood in front of sure hadn't.

Chills ran down my neck and shoulders. This went against everything I had learned so far. Never before had I snuck out of my house, late at night, went in search of a ghost, and found myself in front of a place that could be nothing but haunted. In the light from the streetlamps, I could see the bushes were overgrown, the grass was long and untrimmed, and some of the shutters were tilted as if trying to get as far away from the house as possible.

"Oh, good. You made it!" Rose came bounding out of the house, down the cracked steps and the uneven sidewalk.

"Were you worried I wouldn't make it?" I looked around for werewolves or something that was going to jump out at me.

"Of course not, silly. I got a call about this house. Someone inherited it from their great uncle, and they want me to do a cleanse before they try and fix it up to resell it. Isn't it marvelous?"

I eyed Rose suspiciously. Why was she so cheerful?

"So marvelous."

"Basically, I need you to do what you did last night. Usually, I try to set up the circle where a ghost might wander into it on their usual haunting path, but this one seems a little tricky. I couldn't quite place it. Then I said to myself, I know someone who could help! After seeing what you can do, it's going to be difficult to go back to my old methods."

As we walked, Rose steered me up the sidewalk and into the house. The door squeaked shut behind us, naturally, as we went inside. That was as far as I got because I stopped dead, so to speak, in my tracks.

The house was mostly empty except for a few overturned chairs and random piles of garbage. I could see where Rose had put her candle circle and next to it sat her bag, a crystal, and a rope of hair, like she'd used before.

"Er—how many ghosts can your crystal send back?" I was afraid to move. If just one of those ghosts noticed me, we'd be bombarded with at least seven different spirits. After the library ghost from today had noticed me first, I was terrified other ghosts would do it at as well.

Rose looked at me and where I expected to see alarm on her face, all I saw was excitement. I guess it was possible that some people really did love their jobs. "At least four. Why? Is there more than one ghost here?"

"You could say that." I kept my eyes on Rose, refusing to make eye contact with any ghosts who were milling around. Only one of the many were watching us so far, while the rest of them milled about the spacious living room, the winding stairs, or the back hallway. There could have definitely been more than ten if more ghosts were in the back rooms. "You're going to need at least three crystals, maybe more. I'm not sure I can see them all."

Rose's eyebrows arched in surprise. "Three? Maybe more? I've only brought three, and that's just because I like to keep spares in my bag."

"What can I say? You've sure picked a fun house." I kept the ghost who was watching us in the corner of my eye without looking at him directly. As far as I could guess, he was a teenager, dressed like he was from the 70s, and since he was aware of Rose, I'm sure he'd been the one she was trying to catch who refused to walk into her circle.

Rose bent down and rummaged in her bag. I dared take a few steps in her direction, away from the door, and towards the candle circle.

"I have three crystals, but we have another problem." She turned to me with the first frown I'd seen from her, but she still managed to look elegant and put-together. "I don't have any more binding ropes."

"Oh. Er—do we need to go back to your shop or something? We could come here another time. I'm sure they aren't going to go any-where."

She laughed and waved off my comment with her hand. "No worries. We can take care of this tonight, if you're willing to help."

"Awesome."

"How attached to your hair are you? Besides being literally attached, ha-ha."

"I mean, it's just hair. Right? It'll grow back. How much do you need? I'm not going out of here looking like my head got stuck in a garbage disposal."

"Oh, Hanna. You're so funny. No worries. Would it be okay if I cut it to your shoulders?"

I pulled my honey-colored hair into my fingers and noticed it had grown quite a lot since my last haircut. It wasn't that I was super vain or anything, but I did enjoy having longer hair. "Will you make sure to do a nice job?"

"Of course. I used to cut hair all the time. Besides, it's easy if you're just going straight across." Rose pulled out a pair of scissors from her bag and I wondered how often she went around chopping off people's hair.

"Even in this light?"

"Sure, we'll use the flashlight on my phone."

"And you can't use your own hair?"

"Sadly, no. I have to use someone else's because it's my essence that is wielding the crystal, you see?" She shook her head with a wistful expression. "I wish I could. It would make my life so much easier."

She walked behind me, trailing her fingers through my hair, trying to get it as straight as possible—I could have told her that was pointless.

"Are you sure you're okay with this?"

I nodded. "Yeah, if it means we can get rid of more of... them, then yes. I can sacrifice a few inches for the good of mankind."

"You have no idea how grateful I am." She went to work cutting my hair, and all I could do was stand there, stare at the candle circle, and hope she was doing a good job. A superhero would let her hair be cut if it meant helping others, right?

After she'd carefully gathered my hair, she was able to braid it into four ropes. She put two of them back into her bag, handling them like rare gems, and pulled out two more crystals.

"Okay, do you think we have everything we need?"

"No idea. You're the professional here. As far as I can tell, though, we might have enough supplies to handle just what's in this area."

Rose grinned and grabbed the first crystal, wrapped the hair-that-wasn't-mine around it and nodded to me. "You know what to do. I'll chant. You get them in the circle."

"Right. Cool."

She started chanting and I looked around, not sure what to do first. The one boy ghost was still staring at us from his perch on the highest stair. I suppose he was good looking, or he had been, when he was still alive. He seemed the most aware out of all the ghosts so I figured I could start with him.

Feeling really stupid, I called out. "Hey, you boy. What are you staring at?"

At first the other ghosts ignored me, thank goodness. They probably weren't used to getting many living visitors or paying attention to the world around them.

The boy stood up and took a few steps down the stairs. "What are *you* staring at?"

"I'm staring at someone that shouldn't be here. Come down here so we can get you back to where you belong."

He smirked as Rose kept up her steady chanting. She must have been used to doing it for long periods of time.

"And where do I belong? I've lived in this house my whole life, alive and dead. The house has been in my family for generations. Why must I leave?"

He had a good point, but there was no way I was going to admit that. "You're dead. The dead are supposed to pass on. Don't you want to get on with your existence? Why do you want to stay in a dark, boring old house, anyway?"

He walked down a few more stairs as if considering my words. "How do you know the next place will be better than this one? It could be worse."

I shrugged, faking nonchalance. "Perhaps, but it could be better. Guess that's all up to who you were before you died. Karma and all that."

Two other ghosts had taken notice of our conversation. They were looking at me now and the hairs on the back of my neck were going crazy. It had been a long time since I'd been in the presence of so many ghosts and I had to admit, I didn't like it.

"Why do you care so much anyway?" He walked down a few more steps.

"Er—" I wasn't sure how to answer that, completely unprepared for such candor. "That's just what we do. We help ghosts cross over."

"I've seen a few ghosts cross over in my time." The boy eyed Rose and the circle with a raised eyebrow. "And this looks nothing like it."

Again, I was caught off guard. "Oh, how does it usually look?"

The boy folded his arms across his chest and shook his head. "You really don't have any idea what you are doing, do you?"

"Sure I do. Now get into that circle!" I yelled the last bit with the most commanding voice I could, sick of having an argument with a ghost.

My odd power to command the ghosts must have worked in various strengths, perhaps based on the willpower or amount of energy the ghost possessed. Several of the wandering ghosts looked up in alarm as their feet started pulling them towards the circle. One ghost went so fast, I barely had time to notice it was an old lady in a nightgown.

Rose grew firmer in her chanting and the crystal reached out to the lady ghost with curling pink tentacles and then pulled her in.

I looked back at the boy with a triumphant bob of my head. "See? It's not so bad. Get into the circle!"

A few more ghosts were pulled towards it, but the boy's feet only pulled him down one more stair. He glared at me with determination, but his eyes widened when his feet moved without his consent.

Three more ghosts were zapped by the crystal, and Rose's excited face was illuminated in the pink light. After the fourth ghost went in, she placed the crystal back into her bag, grabbed another and hastily wrapped one of the ropes of my hair around it. All the while, she kept chanting her ritual words, just in case another ghost made it into the circle.

"It's inevitable," I said to the ghost boy, my stare matching his own. "You have to move on. Staying here isn't an option anymore."

One more ghost slid by me. "Help! What's happening?" It was a middle-aged woman, again from the 70s or so, and she was being pulled by the feet towards the circle, dragged by some invisible force as she tried to claw at the wooden floors.

She seemed so desperate I started to feel bad for her. "Don't worry! You're going to another place to pass on. It's just the next step."

Eventually all the ghosts, eight in all, had been pulled to the next life except one. The teenage boy had two more stairs and about six feet left before he was in the circle. We stared at each other.

"Is that all of them?" Rose took a second to stop her chanting.

"There's one more. You were right. This one is stubborn."

"Okay, can't be worse than that ghost from last night." Rose laughed. "Just keep commanding him to go into the circle. I'll keep chanting."

"You heard the lady. Get into the circle!" I pointed again just in case there was any confusion about what I meant.

The boy's lips clamped together in effort and frustration, but his feet slid down the last two stairs. We were even, now, both still staring at each other.

"Do you really think the next life is in those crystals? Where do you think we will go after that? Have you asked yourself that question? Why did she need your hair? Do you really think it was a coincidence that she needed more hair when you were the only one around? You're not the first Seer who's tried to help me. I know what you are, and this is not what your kind do."

His words shook me, and I glanced back at Rose in uncertainty. There did seem to be a lot of coincidences happening. Rose smiled and nodded at me while still chanting, unable to hear the accusations from the ghost boy. Was it possible that this elegant, friendly lady who had been so willing to help me was not sending the ghosts back where they belonged? If they weren't going to the next life, where were they going?

I closed my eyes and took a deep breath. No, the ghost boy was just trying to get me to give up. He was desperate to say anything that would keep him from moving on. Rose had only been nice to me, helping me out when I couldn't get rid of the teacher ghost on my own. She was helping them. She had to be.

"Get into the circle!" I yelled again, opening my eyes.

"You're going to regret this." The boy's iconic words were uttered in a quiet, and almost sad tone as he was finally pulled towards the circle. He kept his eyes on me the whole time until the pink tentacles pulled him away.

Rose and I let out a huge sigh of relief after he was gone, noticed our twin movements, and dissolved into crazed giggles.

"We did it!" Rose cheered.

"I feel exhausted." I rubbed my forehead. "Hopefully, helping you with nine other ghosts more than pays off my debt to you."

"Of course! You were wonderful. I have no idea what I would have done without your help." Rose gathered up her things, carefully storing them into her bag. Her bright smile lit up the dark room.

"Sweet. I'm not sure I'm up for more of that any time soon."

The house was eerily quiet as we left, except for the floorboards that creaked, and the door that squeaked as Rose closed it behind us.

"I'm sure that was difficult for you. I can't imagine. Again, thank you so much."

We walked side by side until we reached the street. The night air was much colder than it had been before, but I was grateful for it as it cooled the sweat on my forehead.

"Do you need a ride home?" Rose asked as she unlocked her car.

"That would be lovely."

"Pardon the expression, but you look dead on your feet."

We both giggled again, although mine was more tired and less exuberant than hers.

My house was dark as she pulled up to it and parked her car across the street.

"Thanks for the ride."

"No, thank you! Seriously, you've helped me more than I can say." Rose had never stopped smiling throughout the whole ride.

"Oh, well, you're welcome. See you around." I got out of the car and shut the door behind me.

She waved cheerfully and then drove away.

I drug my feet towards the back door, let myself in, and snuck back to my bedroom. As I flopped into bed, not even bothering to change into pajamas, I heard Gran's voice.

"And where have you been, young lady?"

There were lots of nice things about having Gran as a ghost. It was nice that I was able to get to know her even though she had passed away when I was young. It was also nice to be able to learn from her.

It was not nice that she could spy on me and keep me in line.

I groaned, rolled over so I could see her, and began to take off my shoes. "I was getting rid of ghosts, like you said to do."

She put her hands on her hips like I'd seen my mother do a thousand times when she was upset with me. The likeness made me want to smile, but I felt too tired for even that.

"I always managed to help ghosts during normal hours."

"Always?" I challenged her with a look.

She sighed. "Fine. Almost always. It's really not safe if no one knows where you are. You never know what could happen."

"Yes, that's true. I'm sorry, Gran. I just needed to help Rose, and I knew Mom wouldn't let me go so late." After taking off my shoes, I flopped back onto my bed to stare at the ceiling. "This one took a lot out of me. I just need to sleep."

She pressed her lips together with a nod. "Sometimes they do that, sweetie. Alright, sleep well, but please promise me you'll be more careful."

"Mmmhmm." I said as I drifted into a haunted sleep.

Chapter 21

Morning sunlight filtered through my window, and I shifted uncomfortably in bed before I remembered I was still wearing jeans. The next thing I noticed was that the house was super quiet. I felt around for my phone which had gotten lost in the blankets.

The clock said it was after ten in the morning. I wasn't sure what to do about that until I opened my text messages and saw one from my mom.

You looked so dead to the world this morning that I just let you sleep. Take the weekend to recover and hopefully you'll be ready for school on Monday. Feel better, dear!

I sighed and flopped back onto my bed and stared at the spackled ceiling. Nights like last night and the one before couldn't keep happening or else my schooling would suffer. All this ghost stuff was starting to catch up with me. These stupid ghosts were ruining my life.

The first thing I did after getting out of bed was take a hot, long shower. It felt refreshing as the water rushed over me, taking away the dirt and yuckiness I felt from the night before.

I couldn't help but recall the words of the ghost boy. Some of the things he'd said felt true, but I desperately didn't want them to be. Having Rose banish the ghosts like that was so much easier than talking to each one, getting their life's story, and trying to help them complete their unfinished business. A project like that could take days, versus the few minutes it took to order a ghost into Rose's circle.

Plus, the implications that Rose was evil scared me. Was I so out of touch with humans that I couldn't tell who was evil and who wasn't? Had I helped an evil person do something horrible to several ghosts?

Nope, I shook my head, letting the water fall into my eyes. Nope, that's not what it was. It couldn't be.

I spent most of the day on the couch while everyone else was gone. It was kind of nice to have the house to myself. Perhaps Mom had been right, and I did need some time to recover from the week's chaos.

At about lunch time, I wandered into the kitchen. I had spent several minutes in front of my mirror after the shower, trying to see if my thighs looked any smaller. I thought that they might have gotten smaller, and my stomach seemed a bit tighter, but they weren't small and tight enough. I had to keep trying to lose the fat.

On the other hand, I was feeling weak. I'd had enough sleep to know *that* wasn't the problem, so I searched the kitchen for something that wasn't fattening but could help me feel less like my head was in a balloon and like my limbs belonged to an 80-year-old woman.

I chewed on my lip as I studied the contents of the fridge. The usual suspects were there, but nothing looked good. My stomach was way past the grumbling stage, merely hollow. I didn't want to eat, but I knew that if I didn't, the weakness would only get worse.

I finally found a bag of baby carrots and munched on one as I looked at my phone. Just as I was about to put it away, it dinged at me, signaling a text message. Then I got one more ding.

It was lunchtime at school and both Andrea and Noah took that moment to text me. I'm sure Noah didn't want her to know he was texting me and the mental image of him turning away from her with his phone perked a small smile.

Are you seriously going to avoid me again, today? Noah said you weren't in class earlier. Don't tell me you stayed home just because you're afraid of me! She ended the message with an eye roll emoji.

The first text was obviously from Andrea and her eye roll made me roll *my* eyes. She really did think the world revolved around her. I decided to read my other messages before responding to hers. If I had sent the first thing that came to my mind, we'd be fighting even more.

Hanna, are you all right? I've been meaning to text you to see if we could find a time to talk... you know, about the weird things.

Oh, great. He wanted to go on more about that weird conversation we'd had. Why was he so persistent in talking to me about all of that? I'd been perfectly normal and sane around him. Mostly.

I decided to play it dumb.

Hey, yeah. I'm fine. Just didn't feel good today so I stayed home. What weird things are you wanting to talk about?

And to Andrea:

I'm not avoiding you. I stayed home sick. I hope you can handle math class on your own again today.

I chewed a few more carrots as I waited for their responses. Carrots weren't my favorite food, but they were low in fat and had a semi-sweetness that wasn't too bad. Plus, I'd heard somewhere they were good for the eyes.

I'm sure I'll be fine. Hope you feel better.

Andrea's lack of friendly emojis said more than words could, and I found myself caring about our friendship again. It appeared that after having dealt with the ghost problems and taken time to rest, I did want to be her friend. We seriously needed some good bonding time if we were going to patch things up.

Thank you (smile emoji) **I hope we can hang out soon. I really don't mind working together on math.**

It was true that I might have been slightly pathetic and should have defended myself more, but I'm terrible at making new friends, and I wanted to keep the ones I had. No friend was going to be perfect. It was about learning and growing together, right?

Cool. We'll see.

That was as much as a response I got, but it was honestly good enough for me. It was going to take time to work through our issues.

In the meantime, Noah had responded: **I really shouldn't say much over texts, but I want to get together in person. We really need to talk. Can we meet for coffee or something?**

Anyone who has had a crush on anyone else knows that if you can get an excuse to hang out with your crush, no matter how weird it might be, you're going to take it. How could I be any different? All I would have to do is keep the conversation out of the weird zone, and we'd be fine.

Sure. I'd like that.

We messaged back and forth until we found a time we were both free, mostly because he had a much busier schedule than I did, and we settled for going out Sunday night.

I was grinning as I put the carrots away and grabbed a bottle of water to take to my room. My mom could come home at any moment since she had such a flexible schedule, and I didn't feel like chatting much with her, or the ghost that followed her.

Plus, I needed to take some time to look over that curse book from the library ghost. She may have mistaken me for someone else and had no idea who I was, or she might have seen something in the future and knew that this exact book was going to help me in some way. The odds were higher for the first, but just in case the latter might be true, it was worth taking a peek.

Noah had responded by the time I'd gotten back to my room.

Perfect! We'll have a good talk. The world may depend on it.

The last bit made me smile because I could imagine him saying that in a funny, sarcastic voice, but I couldn't help feeling an odd premonition that those words might be a tiny bit true, for some reason.

I spent most of Friday evening reading the book on curses and avoiding my family members. Trina tried to come in and talk to me for a sister bonding moment, or whatever, after she'd gotten home from school, but I managed to convince her I wasn't feeling up to it.

Mom and Dad argued downstairs for a while, and usually, I hated the conflict, but I had to admit it was nice because it kept Grandma too distracted from trying to disturb me much. Don't get me wrong, I was enjoying learning from her and was grateful to get a second chance to spend time with her, but sometimes a girl just needed to be able to think and not have to talk to invisible beings only she could see, you know?

I had skimmed through most of the curse book and found it entertaining, if not informative. There were some things inside that I wasn't sure even I believed, and I'd seen a lot of weird crap lately. Like did vampires exist? Sure, ghosts were real, but that didn't mean vampires were. That was a lot harder for me to believe. Witches I could understand, having seen Rose's work. Perhaps she was part witch herself.

At any rate, there were several curses that could affect the supernatural and each curse had a counter-curse that involved various levels of odd items. The ingredients to the counter-curses got me thinking about Rose's shop, and that got me thinking about the banishment from the night before and the uncomfortable words the boy ghost had said before I'd pushed him into the circle.

Perhaps a few follow up questions to Rose would assuage my concerns. It would be awesome if she could clear up the banishment thing better. That 70s ghost was probably desperate to say anything to keep me from helping him get to the next place, for whatever reason. I had no idea why he would want to stay in that creepy old house, but to each their own.

Just before bed, I checked my email and found one from Mr. Tyler. Teachers had access to our email addresses for announcements and the like, but they rarely used them, usually relying on in-class time to say what they needed to. The email was short and sweet, if not a bit weird.

Hanna,

I noticed you weren't at school today and wanted to check in to make sure you were okay. Did something happen with, you know... the other people? Or were you just out with a regular cold? You missed a good discussion today. I hope you are well.

Please let me know,

Mr. Tyler

I was only gone one day. Surely, he couldn't have been that worried about me. Did he send emails like this to everyone who missed a day? That seemed like a lot of work. Ordinarily, I would have ignored the email and just waited to see my teacher on Monday, but Mr. Tyler had seen some odd things and had, so far, proven himself trustworthy, so I figured I could send him a quick email of reassurance.

Mr. Tyler,

I'm fine, just felt worn out from the first week of school, coupled with the chaos of my wonderful gift. I'll be there Monday. Thank you for the concern.

I pushed send and didn't spend another thought on it.

By mid-morning on Saturday, I was ready to face the world again. I took a shower and put on clean jeans and a t-shirt. Saturday mornings were usually a bustle as my dad mowed the lawn and my mom cleaned up the house. It was September, but the grass still grew. I could hear the mower outside while Mom blasted her favorite 80s music from the kitchen as was her usual cleaning routine.

Trina was sitting on the couch with her phone when I came down the hall.

"Hey," I said as I put on my purple jacket.

She looked up and smiled. Even though she was in her pajamas and her hair was mussed from sleeping, she still looked pretty. I don't know why she thought she needed to work so hard to look good. Her natural beauty was stunning.

"I'm glad to see you feel better. Where are you going?"

"Just to this shop I found. It's got some pretty weird stuff that I wanted to check out."

I really hoped she wouldn't ask to go with me. It would be difficult to explain to her why I was interested in all that occult stuff. It would add another reason to the list that her little sister was weird. Plus, it would be difficult to ask the important questions I needed to ask Rose.

Thankfully, she didn't.

"Oh, cool. Let me know if you find anything interesting. Maybe we could go there together sometime?"

I smiled warmly. "Maybe. See ya later!"

"See ya." She went back to her phone, and I went outside.

Dad stopped the mower when he saw me, and I pretty much had the same conversation with him: "I'm glad you're feeling better. Where are you going? That sounds interesting. Let me know what you find out. I'm going to finish up here."

"Sounds great. See ya!" I waved as I set off down the street. It was partly cloudy but warming up for the afternoon. There was a slight cool breeze, but nothing a jacket couldn't handle.

I had tried to avoid thinking about Brandon since I'd seen him last. To be honest, I wasn't very good at it. My thoughts often drifted to him when I didn't have anything more important to think about (and even sometimes when I did). I'd apologized to him, but he hadn't wanted it. I told myself there was nothing more I could do. He might have been dead, but he still had the power to choose some things. If he chose to be mad at me and not want to be my friend, there wasn't anything I could do about it.

As my feet took me towards the skatepark on the way to Rose's shop, I wasn't sure how I felt. I wanted to see Brandon, but I also didn't want to. The awkwardness was almost too much to handle.

The neighborhood was busy with the usual Saturday activity. I passed by a few yard sales with tables boasting loads of used items. My mom loved to check out yard sales and had dragged me on some early Saturday morning trips. Sometimes we found neat things, but most of the time, I was just upset with being awake so early. "You've got to go early to get the good stuff!" she always said.

Cars passed on the street as people went to various ball games for their kids or grocery shopping or whatever good citizens did on Saturday mornings. A ghost stood on the porch of one neighbor's house, and she watched as the kids played in the yard. For the first time, I wondered about her story.

I had always known that each ghost had been a human and that they all had their past lives, but I'd never taken the time to think about that in detail. Each ghost had a story. Gran had told me it was my job to help them complete that story, but the idea of helping so many ghosts do who-knows-what was daunting.

The skatepark was a flurry of activity when I finally got there. Kids were taking advantage of the nice weather. I walked steadily past it, but I couldn't help my eyes from roaming over the cement trying to catch a glimpse of Brandon sliding down a half-pipe or perching on a deck somewhere. I didn't know what I would have done if I had seen him, but I didn't have to figure it out because there was no trace of him in sight.

I felt both relieved and disappointed.

It didn't take long before the houses gave way to small shops. People were walking on the sidewalks as they looked in shop windows and chatted with friends while holding cups of coffee. As I walked up to Rose's shop, I furrowed my eyebrows together in confusion.

A tarp had been draped over the sign and as I got closer, I could see a "FOR RENT" notice in the window. The inside looked dark. There was nothing in the windows on display. No feathers dangling from dream catchers swayed in the air. It simply looked abandoned.

I stood outside the doors for several minutes, studying the empty building. Where had she gone? Why had she left?

Then I remembered she'd texted me and pulled out my phone. I sent her a text and hoped it wasn't too weird.

I went by your shop today, but I see you're gone. Where did you go? Did something happen?

Feeling unsure if she would respond, I Googled her shop name to see if there was a chance she'd just moved locations. There were a few hits, but none of them looked like the Rose's shop that I knew.

As I walked slowly back home, I thought about the words the 70s ghost boy had said. I was sure he would have had something to say about her sudden disappearance.

I was afraid to follow that line of thinking, but I couldn't help it. He'd probably say that she had left because she didn't want me to find out the truth or confront her with the questions I had that might lead to the truth.

But I had helped her trap and find so many ghosts. If that was her aim, for whatever reason, then she would want to keep in contact with me so I could help her find and capture more ghosts, unless she realized I was getting suspicious about the whole thing.

It was also possible that it had nothing to do with me at all, and she'd had to leave to go take care of a sick relative or something.

I kept checking my phone, but she never responded.

The skatepark was the same with no sight of Brandon, and I couldn't help but feel a little lonely. I was surprised at how much I had come to rely on Rose's company in such a short time or how much I wanted to chat with someone like Brandon who was so easy to talk to.

Well, at least there was always my coffee date with Noah to look forward to. The thought of him put a pep in my step, and I made it home just in time to avoid lunch.

Chapter 22

Later that night I had an unexpected visitor that was both creepy and exciting. Those might seem like odd emotions to feel at the same time, but believe me, it's possible.

I was sitting on my bed, scrolling on my phone watching stupid people do stupid things and a couple of makeup videos when I heard a soft tapping on my window.

Even though I was constantly on edge waiting for ghosts to pop up and demand I solve every crisis in the world, not excluding world hunger, inside my bedroom I tended to relax.

My heart jumped inside my chest, and I felt it beating quickly throughout my body as I stared at the closed window blinds. I always kept my blinds closed except for maybe on a rare Saturday afternoon when I wanted to bask in the sunlight. My window faced our backyard which had a few trees and a privacy fence but there were still other houses tall enough that they could see over the fence and through the bushes. If I'd had my window open, who knows how many pervy boys would be able to watch me change.

I slowly got off my bed, unsure of what to do. Perhaps the tap had been my imagination. It could have been a sound from the video I was watching but somehow sounded like it came from my window.

Then the tapping repeated, and my phone was off, discarded to the side of my bed. There was no doubt that the sound was coming from the window.

There weren't any trees or bushes close enough to be causing the sound. It had to be caused by someone doing it deliberately.

"I know you're in there, Hanna. It's just me. Not the boogeyman, I promise," a muffled voice said from the other side. I could tell he was trying to be quiet but still loud enough for me to hear through the window.

"Caleb?" I nearly whispered the words, but he heard through the glass anyway.

"Yes. I just want to talk. Let me inside before your neighbors call the cops."

I frowned, remembering our last interaction, but he was Trina's friend, after all. Even though he was weird, I doubted he would hurt me, but just in case, thanks to the many lectures from my parents about boys, I readied myself with some protection and picked up my phone.

"Okay, I'll let you in, but I've got my phone ready to call for help if you try anything funny." I pulled the string and the blinds shortened, revealing Caleb's handsome face smirking at me through the glass.

"I'm sure that will keep you safe."

I glared. "Do you want to come in here or not?"

He put on a repentant pout, and I found myself distracted by his lips. "I'm sorry. I promise to be good."

Still glaring so he'd know I was serious, I unlatched the window and shoved it upward. There was still a screen between us but with deft fingers, obviously having done this before, Caleb popped it off and leaned it against the outside of the house.

I backed up so he could climb in through the window, and I was impressed by the silence and grace he possessed. If I hadn't been watching him with my own eyes, I would have sworn there was no one there. He was as quiet as a ghost, and I should know.

"I can see that you've done this before."

He chuckled, the sound rumbling deeply from his chest. "Maybe a few times. Why don't you put on some music to cover up our conversation, and so your parents don't figure out you have a boy in your bedroom?"

I couldn't argue with that logic, so I opened my phone and pulled up my favorite music app. I made sure not to turn it up too loud to attract unwanted notice, but loud enough that it would cover up any conversation we could have as long as we stayed in hushed tones.

"Alright, what do you want?"

"Has anyone told you that you have great manners?" His grin was back as he looked around my room.

"My manners are reserved for polite conversation but having a boy sneak into my room at night doesn't seem like a situation for polite conversation. Really, I just want to know why you're here so we can get this over with. Come to tell me again how I should be avoiding my friend? Who, by the way, I've known a lot longer than I've known you." I might have bobbed my head with some attitude, but I'll never admit it.

"Alright, fine. I suppose I can't blame you for the hostility." He twirled my desk chair around and sat down without any invitation to do so. "I'm here because I care. I like what you've done with your hair, by the way."

I rolled my eyes. "Sure. Fine. Whatever. You care. Do you want a badge or something? Why do you care? You don't even know me."

He studied me for a moment, and I found myself tensing under his steady gaze. His brown eyes were illuminated by the soft desk lamp and they were deep pools that drew me in. During the rare moment he was serious, I could see years of pain and a depth in his eyes that surprised me into also being serious. Perhaps he did have something important to say. Perhaps I should at least listen, even if I didn't believe it.

"I know more about you than you think. Do you know why Trina and I are friends? Do you know how long we've been friends?"

Unsure about what it had to do with me, I shook my head. "I think since the first of high school? I don't know. The first time I saw you was like two summers ago? Trina's never told me how you guys met or anything."

"That's about right. We met sophomore year in civics class. I had just moved into the area and your sister was kind enough to invite me to hang out with her friends."

I gave him a pointed look with raised eyebrows. "Kind enough? I'm sure tons of girls were clamoring over themselves to get you to hang out with them."

He at least had the dignity to look a little embarrassed. "Perhaps, but I can read people pretty well and Trina actually meant it. She wasn't trying to get more popular by hanging out with a good-looking guy or use me for her own agenda. She honestly wanted to help me fit in."

"And you could just tell that by talking to her?"

He shrugged. "Like I said, I can read people, and I turned out to be correct. She's as good a friend as any I've had in the past few years. And, I'm right about you, too."

For some reason, his nice words about my sister helped me relax slightly, and I sat on the edge of my bed. "Just because you were right about Trina, doesn't mean you're right about me. We've talked like three times, and all you've learned is I almost got lost on my first day and that my friends make me happy. What is there to be right about?"

"You're more than that. In fact, you're more than what you seem. You're full of secrets, but you're not the only one."

"I know. Noah and his terrible, dark past that proves he will probably murder me some day." I looked at the ceiling and waved my arm around as I sarcastically talked.

"No. I'm talking about me."

"You?" I sat up straighter. "You're actually going to tell me some of your secrets? I tried to get Noah to talk more about you, but he refused."

He nodded his head and pressed his lips in appreciation. "Wow. I have to say I'm impressed with his loyalty. I would have expected someone like him to spill it all to make himself look better. Then again, maybe he didn't want to scare you."

Caleb smiled again, but this time it looked predatory. I swore his canines seemed to grow, but I couldn't be sure in the lighting.

"There is another reason why I wanted to befriend Trina."

"She has nice boobs?"

He rolled his eyes and shook his head. "How shallow do you think I am?"

"About teenage-boy shallow, so very."

He chuckled. "Let's just say that I'm a few years further along than our peers."

"Right." I gave him a look.

"No, the other reason is your family. Your mom's mom is dead, isn't she?"

My heart gave a warning flip in my chest. This conversation was getting too close to the secrets I didn't want to share with anyone, at least not anyone alive who could spread nasty rumors around at school.

"What about my grandma?"

"How much do you know about her?"

"How much do *you* know?" I challenged, unwilling to give an inch.

The corner of his mouth tilted into a half-smile. "Fair. Let's just lay it all out, shall we? All this flitting around the issue is for younger people. I'm too old for this crap."

"Right, because two years older than me is *so* much older."

"Actually, I'm three hundred and seven years old."

My first response was to laugh and shake my head. When he kept staring steadily, waiting for my mind to catch up, I swallowed thickly. "What?"

"You talk to ghosts daily, but you don't think there are other things in the world that may go beyond normal human understanding? Surely you aren't that naïve."

I frowned. "Maybe I am."

"Okay, maybe you are." He shrugged his broad shoulders, making his t-shirt ripple over the muscles underneath. "But you won't be for very long. I know your grandma was a Seer. In fact, I've even talked to her a few times, back in the day."

"How are you that old? You don't look old. What are you?"

"Perhaps that's a discussion for another time."

"You aren't going to suck my blood dry after I foolishly invited you inside my bedroom, are you?"

"Not unless you want me to." The mischievous gleam in his eyes sent shivers down my back but not the scared kind.

My face must have shown some of the shock I was feeling because he laughed. The deep rumble in his chest stirred a reaction inside my belly that wasn't altogether unpleasant.

"Right." I coughed, trying to cover up my discomfort. "Anyway, so you know she was a Seer and you wanted to get close to Trina to see if the power had gone to the next generation."

He nodded, still grinning at me.

"And then you were severely disappointed to find out that she was just an ordinary, albeit attractive, normal teenage girl?"

He shrugged. "Not disappointed, really. Just knew I had to keep looking."

"And then you found me."

"You can see them, can't you? That's why Noah has been so protective of you. That's why he doesn't want me around."

"He's been protective of me? I just thought you guys didn't like each other."

"We don't, but it's more than that. He knows what you are."

"And now you do, too." I frowned again.

He nodded.

"How did Noah find out? I've tried really hard to keep this a secret."

"There's more to Noah than just football."

"I know that, now. Speaking of football, aren't you a little old to be playing it? Heck, aren't you a little old to be in high school?"

"Definitely, but it seemed like a good way to find the next generation's Seer."

"Well, goodie for you. You've figured it out. Now what do you plan to do with the information?"

I wasn't sure I wanted to know what the answer to that was, but since he was in such an honest mood, I'd better try and find out what it was. Maybe Noah had been right to protect me from Caleb. How stupid had I been to let him inside my room? Except... I had a feeling that letting him inside was just a formality. He could have probably gotten in without my help and without me even knowing it, had he wanted to.

Caleb pressed his lips together, studying me. "I've been waiting for some confirmation of what you can do, but since I have it, it just means I'll need to watch over you even more."

"More? Watch over me? From what? Noah?"

Slowly, he shook his head and his eyes gleamed dangerously in the light. "There are much worse things out there than me or even Noah, as bad as his lot is."

Chills rattled down my arms. "What kinds of things?"

He sighed and stood up, brushing the wrinkles out of his jeans from sitting. "Let's just say we have our work cut out for us. It could be a good thing to have Noah's help."

"But why me? What's the big deal about being a Seer?"

"You don't see how being a Seer is so valuable?" He moved closer, and I tensed. "Do you know how many people over the centuries have yearned to talk to the dead? Do you know how many secrets dead people keep? You hold the key to more information than we can even imagine."

My tongue felt dry inside my mouth, and I struggled to speak for a second. "My gran never said anything about all of this. How come she wasn't in danger?"

"Oh, she was. Luckily, she had me."

Then he moved past me and hopped back out my window. As he put the screen in place, he said, "You've been lucky so far, and smart to hide what you can do. Hopefully, we can keep it a secret still until we're better equipped to handle what will come for you."

I was probably as pale as a marshmallow, and he smiled kindly.

"It'll be okay. Luckily, you've got me, too."

Before I could gather enough wits in my brain to respond or figure out what I should do, he was gone, vanishing in the night like he'd never been there. With shaking arms, I shut my window and made sure to lock it tight, but the small metal latch seemed to offer little in the way of protection.

Chapter 23

I spent Sunday morning talking quietly with Gran in my bedroom. Mom loved to sleep in, and she took Sundays as her sleep-in day on the weekends she didn't have photoshoots. Dad usually made a big breakfast for everyone and then spent the rest of the day in front of the TV. Trina, surprise, surprise, spent most of it in her room and then sometimes hung out with her friends in the afternoons.

I'd gotten caught up on my homework and read as much of the curse book as I could for the time being. The content was so heavy and weird, it was going to take me a while to get through the whole thing.

This meant I had time to learn more about being a Seer from Gran and since Rose had disappeared, I finally felt ready to hear what Gran had to say. It also helped that I'd had the conversation with Caleb, and he had gotten me thinking about what other creatures were out there and how much did Gran know.

Also, the words from the ghost boy I had banished with Rose still echoed in my head. I owed it to him to at least learn more about helping ghosts cross to the other side, you know, just to make sure I'd done it right with Rose. If I had done something wrong I was going to need to make things right.

"Okay. Let's start from the very beginning. When was the first time you saw a ghost?" I had even gotten out a pen and paper in case there were any important notes I needed to take.

Gran sat on the chair next to my desk. Her hands were folded in her lap on top of the calf-length, blue housecoat she always wore. I had assumed that the clothes a ghost was stuck wearing was whatever they had worn when they'd died. I hoped that when I died I wasn't wearing something ridiculous.

She tilted her head back and studied the ceiling for a moment. "Let's see. I was thirteen, I think."

"Wow, that seems late. I was four."

Her eyebrows rose in surprise. "That was early. That's the earliest I've ever heard of."

"And how many Seers have you heard of?"

"It seems to skip a generation. My grandmother Effie was also a Seer. She taught me everything I know and as much about the past Seers as she could. According to her, the powers always manifested during adolescence."

"Huh. Great. Another weird thing about me."

Gran showed me a patient smile. "Or another great thing about you. When I was thirteen, I was working at a local dress shop after school. One day I was in the back room organizing the bolts of fabric and cleaning up, when as clear as you please, an old lady walked right through the wall and started ordering me around. She wasn't talking to me, as you probably can guess, but rather someone in her memory, but I didn't know that. All I knew was that there was this transparent blue lady barking orders at me. I had heard stories from my grandmother about ghosts before that. You see, she'd guessed that one of her granddaughters would manifest with the Seer gift and made sure to tell us all stories about the ghosts so we'd know a little of what to expect and also know who we could go to talk to about them."

"That was nice of her, as long as the stories weren't too scary."

"They weren't too scary, just a little." A wistful smile stayed on Gran's lips as she kept telling her story. "I knew it was a ghost, but like I said, didn't realize she wasn't talking to me. She told me to make sure to scrub the floors until they were so clean, we could eat off of them, and then I was to go out to market and find more thread."

"So, she was a ghost who worked at the dress shop before?"

"Yes, I later found out she was Rachel's, the woman I worked for, great aunt who had founded the shop. That store was her life's legacy, and she haunted it in death to make sure the place kept running correctly."

"So, what did you say when you thought she was talking to you?"

"Oh, I'm sure you know the moment well, but when a Seer talks to a ghost, they seem to wake up and realize they are in a different world than the one in which they were alive. They don't always realize they're dead and ghosts, though."

"I know the exact moment you're talking about. It's both terrifying and pretty cool."

"It is. Well, I asked her what color of thread she wanted me to get, and she had that moment. Once she woke up, she was confused. The shop had changed a lot since she'd been there, you see. She also had no idea who I was or what I was doing in her store. Luckily, I had remembered my grandmother's stories, and I realized what was happening. Rule one, my grandmother said, was to remain calm and kind."

"That's hard to do in the face of a ghost, especially an angry one throwing books at you."

"Oh, definitely, but your panic or anger will only escalate the situation. You need to treat them like they're a scared, but dangerous, animal."

"Makes sense."

"I told her who I was and who I worked for. The familiar name of her great niece seemed to help calm her down. Of course, I didn't tell her that her niece was now almost seventy years old, but it always helps to start with the familiar, if you can. You've got to ease them into the new world a little at a time."

"I remember you telling me that the other day. I really messed that up with the teacher ghost." And about a dozen more, I thought to myself, not quite ready to share with her about the haunted house I had helped banish with Rose.

"Yes, it can lead to unfortunate circumstances. At any rate, I managed to help her realize she was dead. That was the most I knew to do at the time until I could talk to my grandmother again and get further instructions."

"And what did great-great grandma say after that?"

"It took me a little while to get a hold of her as she was traveling, and we didn't have cell phones back in those days. So, this ghost lady became my companion, of sorts, for a few weeks while I worked in the store. She kept a close eye on everything that was happening and would always try to correct someone to do it her way. I sometimes tried to give her suggestions to the people that were alive and a few times, they listened to me and fixed the issue. Actually, one time I told Rachel to fix the way she was hemming a dress and she looked up at me with the biggest eyes. She'd told me that was the exact way her grandmother had taught her to hem, and she'd forgotten the technique. Of course, I couldn't tell her that's exactly who was telling me how to fix it."

"Wow. I bet you freaked her out."

"And that was far from the last time I did that to somebody."

I smirked. "I'm sure."

"When I finally got a letter back from my grandmother, she was so excited for me. It was kind of funny, actually, how happy she was that I could see ghosts."

"Maybe because she wasn't the only one anymore?"

"Maybe. Anyway, her letter told me to get to know the ghost and find out why she was stuck and not passing beyond."

"How did you feel about doing that? It seems kind of scary."

Gran smiled kindly at me. "I know it can seem scary. I was a little scared, at first, too, but I took it slowly and it wasn't too long before we were chatting like old friends, only when I was alone in the back room, of course. Didn't want people thinking I was crazy or something."

I grinned. "Of course not."

"So eventually, after a few months or so, I was able to get to know her better and find out more about her life and death. It turned out that she really wanted her store to be successful. If I could somehow get her to feel that it was, she'd be able to pass beyond with ease."

"How did you do something like that?"

"I managed to convince Rachel to have a big event where we put tables outside with displays of our most beautiful dresses. I got some balloons and made some fresh cakes. One of the other girls made some homemade lemonade. We planned it on a Saturday when the boardwalk would be as busy as possible. We worked for months to get it ready, sewing extra dresses and investing money into new and better fabrics. I hyped up the event to the ghost and told her all about it. Of course, she watched us work very hard on the dresses and saw how much effort we put into it. She saw how much we all cared about the success of the shop. The day of the event finally came and solidified to her that the shop was in good hands. We had so many ladies looking at dresses, we weren't even able to talk to all of them. It was an amazing turnout. I'll never forget the image of this old lady ghost peering out the window of her shop in awe as so many people looked at the dresses we'd made. We didn't quite sell all the dresses, but we had so many people looking and had many future orders set up that we all felt it was quite successful."

"Was the old lady ghost able to pass beyond then?"

"It took another conversation that night, actually. I went back to the store just before sunset. It was already closed, but I stood outside and looked in through the window at a wedding dress we'd had on display. The ghost stood on the other side, and we talked about how successful the day was. It took a solemn promise on my part that we would look after the store and we'd never let her down, but she finally agreed to go."

"Wow. That was a lot of work."

"Definitely, but not all of them take that much. Sometimes it's not much work at all and they just need a shoulder to cry on for a while. It depends on what's happened."

I rubbed my eyes, feeling somewhat overwhelmed. "And as a Seer we're supposed to do that for *every* ghost we see?"

Gran reached over and patted my hand, or tried to. It went right through, but I appreciated the gesture. "Don't think of it like that. It's too much work to expect you to do it all."

"You're telling me."

"But you try your best. That's all we can do."

"Are there any other ways to help a ghost besides talking to it and helping it do its unfinished business?"

"Are you talking about that banishment stuff that your friend did on the teacher ghost?"

I nodded, still worried I'd messed up somehow.

"As far as I know, it's the only way. I've never heard of a banishment like you described. I guess I would have to see it for myself to know more. I do know, however, that talking to the ghost is the best way to help them. At least you know they are at peace and have passed on to the next place where they are meant to be. With this banishment deal, how do you know they got where they were supposed to?"

"I guess you don't."

She nodded, studying my face. "I know it can be scary and completely overwhelming but think of it as a gift, something you can give to help people. Some are given gifts to inspire or teach or comfort. You've been given a gift to help restless souls pass on. It's such a rare thing, and you should be proud of it."

"I want to be proud of it. I want to be comfortable with it."

"It'll come in time, dear. Just take it slow. One step at a time. One day you'll look back and be surprised at the progress you've made while taking one step at a time."

"Okay. I'll try, and you'll help me?"

"Absolutely."

We fell quiet for a moment, and I had no idea what my Gran was thinking about, but the last comments had me wondering. "What do you think your unfinished business is? I want to say it's to help me with all this Seer stuff, but that would mean you would haunt me, right? How come you are haunting Mom? And how come you aren't stuck in one place like other ghosts are? Have you ever seen someone haunt another person before?"

Gran laughed and raised her hands up in surrender. "Woah, there. That's a lot of questions. One step at a time, remember?"

"Okay, fine. How come you're haunting Mom?"

Gran sobered and looked at me thoughtfully. "That's the hard part about being a ghost and why we need Seers. It's difficult to exactly pin down what our unfinished business is. It's not like we're given a pamphlet or anything. It's more like an uneasy feeling of obsession looms over us. Sometimes it's easy to pinpoint and other times, it isn't. I've met lots of ghosts who were hard to help because it took a while to figure out what they needed."

"Awesome."

"It can be a struggle, but it's not so bad. It feels good when you can help a ghost move beyond, it makes it all worth it."

That last sentence swirled around in my head the rest of the after-noon. I chewed on my pen while doing homework and thinking about how it would feel to help a ghost move beyond. It would probably feel better the older the ghost was or the longer the ghost had been dead. Again, I wondered about Brandon and what his business was.

There were at least two ghosts I didn't want to get rid of, though, and for me, that was quite different from what I had thought a mere week ago.

Chapter 24

Nerves fluttered through me as I got ready for my coffee date with Noah. To assuage my nerves, I kept telling myself to stop thinking of it as a date, and instead, dwell more on the fact that it was probably going to be a weird conversation about things I didn't want to talk about. Not to mention, after talking with Caleb last night, he had convinced me that I needed to be more careful with who I hung out with. I tried to focus on these negativities, but it didn't work. Even if we were going to talk about the migration of sea slugs, I was still excited to spend any time with Noah alone.

Trina meandered into the bathroom after I had finished using the blow dryer. "Where are you going?"

As I ran my fingers through my hair, trying to get used to the shortness of it and to distribute smoothing oil to the ends, I looked at her in the mirror. "Somewhere your friend Caleb wouldn't want me to be."

"Caleb? Are you referring to his weird warning about Noah? Wait—are you hanging out with Noah today?" Her eyes got big and excited as she knew how much I liked him. She was wearing a t-shirt and sweats but had still made time to put on some eyeliner and mascara.

I grinned, unable to suppress my excitement. "We're going out for coffee."

She squealed and jumped up and down on her toes.

I laughed. "It's just coffee."

Immediately, she grabbed a brush and attacked my hair. "This is tricky. We need to make you look as cute as possible, but also like you weren't trying too hard with it being a Sunday afternoon. Like I said the other day, I'm still not sure why you decided to cut your hair so short. It seems like a rather quick decision to make for a situation so important."

I shrugged, unsure what to say.

She easily filled the silence for me. "Sometimes you just need a change, I suppose. I've almost cut my own hair off before. Luckily I came to my senses."

"Thank goodness."

"It's all good. You just leave it to me, girl. We got this."

I was glad I'd started getting ready early because Trina needed every bit of an hour just to do my hair and makeup. I found it quite ridiculous, but I was also grateful for her help. By the time she was finished, I had to admit I looked super cute but also casual and effortless.

Looking effortless took a lot of effort.

"Ta-da!" she said as she finished putting the last coat of mascara on my eyelashes. "You look great! I wish you'd let me help you every day for school. All the boys would be clamoring for your attention, every day. Maybe even some of the teachers." She said the last bit with a wink.

"Uh, no thanks. We'd have to get up three hours early to get the both of us done in time for first period."

She laughed and nodded. "That's probably true."

"Thanks for helping me." I smiled at her in the mirror.

"Of course!"

We hugged, which was rare for us, but I had to admit it was nice.

Of course, Mom had forty questions for me before I could take a step out of the house, but after I had assured her several times that we were just going for coffee and I wouldn't be out too late, probably back home before it even got dark, she finally stopped interrogating me.

I had high hopes for the afternoon as I stepped out onto our porch, even though it was cloudy and a bit grey. The wind had picked up and was bringing a deep chill with it.

As I looked towards the road, I was surprised to find Mr. Tyler standing on the sidewalk in front of our house. A red truck I didn't recognize was parked on the street behind him, and I figured it must have been his.

"Ah," he took a deep breath and closed his eyes to savor the clean air. "That's the stuff."

"Mr. Tyler? What are you doing here?"

The prickles on the back of my neck were trying to warn me about something, but I couldn't figure out what it was. Mr. Tyler wasn't a ghost. He was my teacher and had proven to be trustworthy, keeping my weird secrets, and even helping me banish a ghost. Why was my intuition suddenly screaming that I should run away?

"Hmm. That's a good question. It does appear quite odd that I would show up at your house right now, uninvited, unexpected. On that note, do you mind if I stick around for a bit? Perhaps you could invite a poor soul in for some tea?"

"Where do you think you are? The British countryside?" I said it with a smile so he would know I wasn't trying to be rude. "Actually, I would invite you to meet my parents, but I'm on the way out. Could we schedule it another time? Is there something urgent you need to tell them? I promise I'll make up the work from Friday that I missed."

He waved his hand in the air nonchalantly. "No, it's nothing like that. No need to worry yourself. I was just enjoying your company. There's something about you that really feeds a hungry soul, you know?"

The neck prickles zinged down into my back. What was he talking about? Those were odd words coming from an alive person. I might have tolerated them coming from a ghost, but Mr. Tyler was alive. At least, I was pretty sure he was. I was certain others could see him, so he couldn't have been a ghost. The easier (and less creepy... kind of?) answer was that he had a weird, old-man crush on me, but I'd never heard rumors about Mr. Tyler being a pervert or anything.

Hah, I know, I sound so silly, but I didn't know what else to think.

"I'm not sure what you mean, exactly, but I'm late to go meet with someone so I'll see you tomorrow in class." I walked through my yard towards the sidewalk, but at an angle, not towards Mr. Tyler who was still standing next to his truck.

"Can we just talk for a few more minutes? I really need the energy."

"What energy? What are you talking about?" I kept edging away from him, hoping he'd get the hint.

He shook his head and laughed. "You really are clueless. Have you not noticed that ghosts get stronger in your presence?"

"I mean, I guess. What does that have to do with you?"

"I can feel it."

"Good for you. Still got to go. See you tomorrow!"

I turned to leave and head down the street, but he moved faster than I've ever seen a normal human do and grabbed my arm above the elbow.

"Hold on! Just hang out with me for a minute more." He smiled but it wasn't the usual, teacher-like smile I'd seen from him at school. This smile felt sinister and creepy.

"Let me go!" I pulled to get away from him, but his grip was strong, more like iron than human flesh and blood.

"What's happening out here?" Gran's ghost fazed through the walls of the house and came outside. "Who is this?"

Mr. Tyler couldn't have known she was there, but he paused, looked around like he was smelling something and looked in Gran's direction. "Ah, I should have known you'd have more around you. Mmmm." He took a deep breath. "Even more energy. Love it."

"What are you talking about?" I yanked hard with my arm and was rewarded with its freedom. "You don't seem like yourself. Did something happen, Mr. Tyler?"

A weird gleam shone in his eyes. "No. It's nothing new."

"Have you been possessed?" I whispered the absurd question.

Gran took a few more steps towards us but she slowed and clutched at her head. "Oh, I don't feel so good."

"Are you doing something to her?" I looked between Mr. Tyler and Gran. His indulgent smile was enough of an answer. "What are you doing?"

"I haven't been possessed, dear. I know who I am and am in complete control of my own body, except, well, for one thing. I just really crave this kind of energy. I can't explain it much beyond that, and it was manageable as long as I had that ghost in my classroom. For some reason, being around ghosts makes me feel good."

I blinked, trying to process what he was saying. How was this possible? He was alive. He was human (probably), and yet something inside of him craved ghostly energy. And from the looks of Gran, he was able to steal it, somehow, and pull it into himself. Words from the book I'd been studying all weekend surfaced into my mind as I considered his situation.

"Have you been cursed, Mr. Tyler?"

He shrugged, took another deep breath, and moved closer towards Gran. She bent over with her hands on her knees and had she needed to breathe, I got the feeling she would have been panting heavily.

"Stay away from her!"

"But she smells so good."

I put myself between them and gave Mr. Tyler a light shove in the other direction. "You can feed off me, if you have to, but leave my gran alone."

"She's your grandma? Aw, that's cute."

"Something is wrong," Gran said behind me, her voice weak.

"Stop feeding on her! You're going to take all her energy!" I gave Mr. Tyler another shove.

He was stronger than his wiry form should have been, but I didn't know whether that was how he was usually, or if it was a part of the curse. "I don't mean to hurt her, but it feels so good."

His eyes were clouded and unfocused as he stared vaguely in her direction. I glanced back at Gran and saw her blue form fade and flicker a few times.

"Stop it! Leave her alone!" I put my hands on his chest, dug my cute shoes into the grass, and pushed, trying to get him further away, in case some distance would help.

"You're getting really annoying!" He growled and pushed me to the side like I was a leaf in the wind.

"Hanna, it's okay. I can—"

But Gran didn't get to finish her sentence before she winked out of sight.

"Gran!"

"Hmm... That didn't last as long as I wanted. Oh well, at least I still have you to draw from." Mr. Tyler focused his face back in my direction, although his eyes still didn't make contact.

Sprawled out on the grass, distantly wondering if I was getting grass stains on Trina's jeans she'd let me borrow, I tried to remember which curse he had and how to get rid of it. I was kicking myself for not memorizing every word in that spooky book.

"How can I help?" Brandon popped up next to me, kneeling in the grass with earnest eyes.

"Gah!" I fell back further onto the grass. "Brandon! How did you get here?"

Mr. Tyler again looked around and inhaled. "Ah, another one. I knew coming here would be a good idea. You're like a ghost gold mine."

"Oh, he's creepy. What's going on?" Brandon glanced back and forth between me and my crazed teacher.

"I—I think he's cursed? He did something to my grandma." I wished I could say I was talking calmly and with brave composure but really, I was shaking and scared. I'd never seen anything like it. "You need to get out of here before he does something to you!"

Mr. Tyler was only three or so feet away from me at that point, and I didn't want him to get any closer.

"I knew there was something special about you. You're the first student I've ever had who noticed the ghost in the classroom. Even though I had found him useful for energy, I wanted to see more of what you could do so I let you banish him." Mr. Tyler frowned slightly as he remembered. "Unfortunately, I underestimated how terrible I would feel without him, or you, apparently, inside my class every day. When you missed Friday and then I had to face going all weekend without the energy, I had to get here to grab another fix."

Even though I was confused and scared, my brain was still trying to make sense of the situation. Somehow, I was able to process his words and try to figure out what was happening.

"So, you siphon energy from ghosts and people?" It felt weird to ask him questions about his odd state, and even weirder to expect him to answer, but I needed more information to figure out what curse I needed to break and how to do it.

"Oh, no, not all people. That would be so much easier. Like I said, you are special." He took another deep breath through his nose and closed his eyes to savor whatever it felt like to pull ghostly energy from something.

"Yup, definitely creepy."

"Brandon, you need to get out of here! He could take you like he took Gran. It's not safe!"

"Oh, a boy ghost and you know his name. How cute."

"He's been taking energy from that teacher ghost for years and he always came back. I'm sure she'll come back, too," Brandon said with a firm nod as if he were an expert.

"I don't want to take that chance. You need to leave. Now. Please don't make me command you to leave," I not only pleaded with words but also with my eyes, hoping he'd listen, for once.

He didn't.

"But you need my help!"

"No, I don't! I don't need help from ghosts!" I screamed the last part, pouring all of my passion, fear, and anger into the words so I could free them from inside.

Instead of getting angry with me and disappearing like I wanted him to, Brandon only smiled. It wasn't his usual smirk or teasing grin. It was a kind, compassionate smile that I didn't know what to do with.

Mr. Tyler was laughing, probably at my exchange with an invisible being he couldn't hear or see but could definitely distinctly feel. "Wow! You're a hot mess, aren't you?"

"If you didn't need help from ghosts, then how are you going to break this curse?" Brandon turned away from me and reached out to the grass, clutching at something I couldn't see until he touched it. With a sharp tug, he revealed a thick chain made of whatever makes up ghosts, ghost plasma, I guess. It wrapped around and through Mr. Tyler's chest and stomach, clamped together with a giant lock, and then trailed down his body, to the ground, through the grass, and off into the distance towards some unknown destination.

"What's that?" I leaned over and tried to grab the chain, but of course, I couldn't.

"I'm guessing it's the curse. Can you see the energy pulsing from him down through the chain?" Brandon dropped it and dusted off his hands as if having just touched something dirty.

"I can't see that. I couldn't even see the chain until you touched it." I gathered my legs beneath me and they wobbled as I stood, but at least they held me up.

There was Brandon's teasing grin. "See? You need me."

I sighed and shook my head. "You'd be more helpful if you could break this curse."

Brandon studied the chain and tapped his chin in thought while I turned back to Mr. Tyler.

"How did this happen? Who did this to you?"

Mr. Tyler shrugged. "How does anything happen? All I know is it just feels so good."

"Helpful."

Even after Brandon had let go of the chain, I could still see it. Somehow, his contact with it had revealed its presence to my senses. This whole ghost power thing was more complicated than I'd ever considered. As I looked at the chain curling around my teacher's body, my mind finally recalled something I'd read from that book.

"It's different from the picture, but I'm thinking this could be the *residuam* curse." I was sure I pronounced the word incorrectly but talking aloud helped me gather my thoughts. It was a slow drain, but I had started to feel the effects of Mr. Tyler's pull. Earlier, he'd taken straight from Gran, but once she'd disappeared, he began to take directly from me. Brandon didn't seem affected by the curse at all. He wasn't getting weaker or fainter. Perhaps it was because I was sustaining Brandon while Mr. Tyler took energy directly from me instead of aiming at the ghost like he'd aimed at Gran. It probably also didn't help that I hadn't really eaten much in the last week. My body felt weaker and fainter than I'd ever felt before.

I was light-headed, dizzy, and aware of a gnarly headache beginning to build in the back of my skull. On one hand, I was grateful that Brandon was going to be fine, as long as I could break the curse before Mr. Tyler drained me completely. On the other hand, my head was throbbing, and I didn't like it, not even a little.

"I'm sure that's how you *not* say it," Brandon teased as he bent down to pick up the chain again. He gave it a good tug, but it held firm. Mr. Tyler didn't even move from the force. "How do we get rid of it?"

"I remember reading somewhere that we need a special dagger, but for curses using ghost plasma stuff like this one, the book called it *plasmara*, the dagger needs to be made of the same stuff or it won't work. It's like they're from different dimensions or something."

"Hmm." Brandon tapped his lip again and studied the chain.

In what felt like a backwards hurricane, Mr. Tyler took another deep breath, his eyes locked onto mine, and *pulled*. "Somehow, it just never feels like enough. I need more!"

Energy flowed out from my hands and feet. The pull was so strong, I could physically feel it. Was this what Gran had felt moments ago? How had I allowed such torture to happen?

"I don't feel so good." I flopped to my knees into the grass. It was cool and dry compared to the whirling around me. Blackness edged in on the sides of my vision, and it was the most I could do to keep breathing.

"Hanna!" I heard Brandon's shout like I was underwater and he was far away. "Hold on!

In my foggy delirium I saw another car was suddenly parked behind Mr. Tyler's and someone who looked like Noah stepped out. He looked around and then ran to me as I was hunched over.

"Hanna? I figured I could offer you a ride so you didn't have to walk. Are you okay? What's Mr. Tyler doing here?" Noah's hazel eyes peered at me through the fog. I used them as a focal point.

"I don't know. I have a really bad headache." I squinted and my eyelids trembled. "Are you really here?"

Mr. Tyler took another deep breath, and I swayed with the pull on my energy. His laughter drove Noah's eyes towards him, and the football player stood, his stance turning defensive.

"What are you doing to her?!"

Mr. Tyler kept laughing. "Of course, a necromancer would be interested in a Seer. What are you trying to use her for this time? Did someone get murdered too soon?"

I blinked slowly as my brain tried to process the confusing words.

"At least I would never hurt her! What are you doing?!" Noah strode towards Mr. Tyler purposefully.

The teacher put his hands up in surrender. "Woah. It's fine. Not doing anything she won't recover from. I should probably get going anyway. It's a school night, after all."

"You're not going anywhere," another person spoke through the fog. His voice was deeper, authoritative and somehow, oddly compelling.

"Geez, how many boyfriends do you have?" Brandon put his hands on his hips as he appraised Caleb who had apparently popped out of nowhere, just like a ghost.

"Wait—Don't hurt him!" I called out weakly.

It was probably the fog making everything seem like it was moving too fast, but Caleb had basically teleported from one place on the grass to standing right behind Mr. Tyler. His powerful dark arms were placed strategically around my teacher's head in a stance I had seen in movies right before someone breaks another person's neck.

Mr. Tyler was no longer laughing, his eyes wide, and it struck me as odd to see my teacher, an authority figure, in such a powerless state. It was even odder when I could have sworn his hands were growing into wicked claws and dark fur was sprouting down his arms.

"What are you doing here?" Noah nearly growled at Caleb. "You can't just go around killing people who get in your way!"

"Why not? We both know he's not a human. Plus, you'd just raise him up again. Wouldn't it be neat to have a super cool werewolf pet?" Caleb's smirk was confident and mocking.

"He's cursed. He's not himself." My voice was weak, but they must have heard me. Both turned their gazes toward me.

Mr. Tyler was writhing in Caleb's stone grip, but it didn't seem to matter much. Caleb's muscular arms bulged with the effort of keeping a strong werewolf (I guess??) from breaking free.

"Hanna, he's hurting you. We have to stop him," Caleb said calmly and firmly, as if talking to a young child.

Clearly in pain, a growl rumbled deep in Mr. Tyler's throat. I wasn't sure if it was from Caleb's impressive hold or the change of fur rippling over Mr. Tyler's skin.

"Just break the curse," I nearly whispered. It was difficult to keep my head up, let alone project my voice for anyone to hear.

"Looks like these meatheads only know one answer to problems. Violence isn't the answer, kids!" Brandon was joking about the situation, but his eyes kept darting back to me in concern. Joking was probably all he knew to do when he was just a useless ghost.

Caleb slowly let go of Mr. Tyler's head and snarled harshly into his ear, "Don't think you're safe, wolf. I can snap your neck before you take a blink."

Growling and snarling, Mr. Tyler dropped to his hands and knees. I'd never seen claws so wicked or teeth so sharp and he wasn't even fully transformed yet. Somehow, as Caleb let him go, Mr. Tyler's shuddering form seemed to gain more control and the hair began to recede.

"What's happening?" I blinked through the haze, trying to figure out if all this was real or if I was hallucinating from fatigue.

Noah and Caleb kept sharp eyes on our teacher waiting to see what his next move would be.

"He's smart to change back to human. We are in the middle of the day, in a quiet neighborhood, nowhere near the full moon," Caleb muttered, looking around for anyone who might have been looking out of their window.

Brandon was studying the chain. He'd picked it up again and was tugging on it, pulling on it, and feeling along the links for any weak ones.

After a few minutes, Mr. Tyler collected himself and even though his legs were shaking slightly, he was able to stand. "I'm sorry. I didn't mean to lose so much control. I think I'd better get going."

"We might not get to kill you, but we can't just let you go, either." Noah put himself between Mr. Tyler and his truck.

"Hanna, do you know how to break the curse?" Caleb asked me, keeping his eyes trained on our teacher.

"I'm not sure. There's some kind of chain made of ghost matter, plasma, or whatever that's called. If we can break the chain, then maybe it will break the curse?" It was a hoarse whisper, but they must have been able to still hear me. My head had started to clear a little as Mr. Tyler was distracted.

"The easiest way is to kill him," Caleb muttered, but at least he didn't try to grab his head to snap his neck again.

"You're lucky you're not in my classes anymore." Mr. Tyler was breathing heavily. "I'd flunk you for that statement. Look, kids, it's fine. I promise not to cause any more trouble. I just need one more drag to get me through the night." Mr. Tyler inhaled again.

The world spun and grew dark. The last thing my mind registered was that Noah had a sharp object held against Caleb's chest that looked suspiciously like wood, blocking him from murdering Mr. Tyler while Brandon was preoccupied searching the pockets of his giant pants.

Chapter 25

I must have blacked out for several moments because the next thing I remember was feeling very crowded and embarrassed as three faces hovered over mine with worried expressions.

"Hanna? Can you hear me?" Brandon peeked in between Noah and Caleb.

"Oh, good. She's awake." Noah was to the right.

Caleb was to the left. "Are you okay?"

The early evening sun turned the sky pink above their heads, and I tried to focus on that instead of the fact that there were too many boys sitting way too close to me. Or were they boys? One was a ghost, and I only had suspicions about what the other two were, although it was clear they weren't 100% human. It takes talent to make so many odd friends.

"What happened?" I was still groggy and slurring my words.

"Don't try to sit up. Just breathe for a moment." Noah pushed gently on my shoulder as I tried to get up.

I wanted to ignore his advice and get away from all the scrutiny, but my head hurt so badly, I slumped back into the cool grass anyway. "Vampires, and werewolves, and necromancers, oh my," I said groggily, the words still slurring.

Caleb grinned and Noah flinched.

"As much as I hate to admit it, I agree with the necro. Just relax." Caleb's breath smelled like mint, and I caught a whiff of frost that brought a dark stranger immediately to my mind. Memories flooded in of that terrible night, and my mind spun with the possibilities. He had said he had helped my gran... I'd have to worry about that later.

There was too much on my mind already.

Brandon hovered behind the guys, wringing his hands, and glancing back at Mr. Tyler's body which was laying in the grass motionless.

"Is he dead?" I asked, my heart sinking in fear.

"Not dead. His heartbeat is strong." Caleb glanced at Mr. Tyler with a confused look. "But I'm not sure what happened. One minute he was breathing, sucking in your ghost energy, the next minute he was on the ground sleeping like a baby."

"No thanks to you." Noah snarled at Caleb. "This creeper was going to murder him."

Caleb threw his shoulders up in a shrug. "It seemed like the only way to get him to stop hurting Hanna. You wanted him to stop hurting her, right?"

Noah and Caleb locked eyes in a staring contest while my gaze moved to Brandon who was sighing and shaking his head.

"What actually happened is that I remembered I died with my pocketknife in my pocket. I figured if I could find it, it would be the plasma knife needed to sever the chain. It must have worked because the chain snapped clean apart after I sawed at it for a moment. Then it disappeared, and your teacher fell to the ground."

"Huh," I commented elegantly.

Noah broke off the glare from Caleb and looked back at me. "Do you want to try and sit up now?"

I nodded, and with their help, I could at least sit in the grass, even if I wasn't ready to stand yet. "So now what? Should we call the police or wait for him to wake up or what?"

"Ugh, right, authorities." Caleb frowned in distaste. "That's my cue to get out of here."

"Yeah, you probably want to go crawl back into your coffin or something," Noah said.

Before we could give Caleb a proper goodbye, Trina walked out of the front door and paused on the porch. "Why are you sitting there in the grass? Why are they looking at you like you just died? Wait—is that Mr. Tyler? Is he okay?"

Trina jogged to our teacher's body as it lay in the grass near the road. She kneeled to check his pulse and sat back on her heels after a few moments, satisfied he was still alive. He must have looked human enough that she wasn't freaked out, which sent a small swirl of relief through me. "What happened out here? Does he need a doctor?"

Caleb stood and dusted a few strands of grass off his designer jeans. "He's probably okay. Might not hurt to call an ambulance, though."

"Probably? What are you doing here, anyway?" Trina let Caleb pull her up off the grass.

"I was just passing by and saw your sister feeling a little faint. I figured I'd check in to see if she was okay."

Trina's gaze shifted to take a better look at me. "Hanna? What's wrong? Are you okay? What is happening?!"

"I'm okay. Mr. Tyler came over to check on me since I missed school on Friday. Then he seemed to get woozy and kind of just fell over. We should call an ambulance for him. Do you know if he's diabetic?" The words flowed out of my mouth better than I'd expected, surprising me.

Brandon shook his head slightly. "You're not a very good liar, are you?"

I ignored him and tried to give Trina a reassuring smile. It must have wavered some because she didn't fully believe me.

"But why are you sitting in the grass looking paler than Mom in the winter? Have you been eating?" Trina put her hand on my forehead as if to check my temperature.

"Sympathy pains?" I shrugged with a smile.

Noah gave my sister a reassuring nod. "She's okay. She's just resting for a moment."

Trina shook her head and pulled out her phone. "You both probably need to get checked out. Hello? Yes, we need an ambulance at twenty-seven Oakwood Street. Our teacher passed out and we don't know why."

Brandon, Noah, and I watched Trina be an adult and do the responsible thing. It was probably a good idea since I had no idea what effects breaking the curse would have on Mr. Tyler nor did I feel like I was exactly thinking straight.

Caleb disappeared without saying goodbye to any of us. He was there one second, and then after Trina called for help, he was gone. I had no idea how he'd managed to leave so fast without a car, but I attributed the confusion to my addled brain.

"Who would and could put a curse on someone like that?" Brandon said a few minutes later.

Both Brandon and Noah sat next to me on the porch as we watched the EMTs administer to Mr. Tyler. Trina and my parents (brought out by the ambulance siren) hovered near the authorities, trying to answer any questions they might have.

I couldn't answer Brandon's question outright, but I could talk about it with Noah. He had said I could share with him, and it seemed like a good time to start as any.

"How did Mr. Tyler get cursed like that? In a book I recently found, kind of, it talked about witches and voodoo priests and satanic worshippers and all kinds of people who knew how to do stuff like that. I'll have to go back and see if there is more information about that specific curse." I fiddled with the strands of my hair as I thought.

Noah took his eyes off the scene in front of my house and turned to look closely at me. I felt warm under his scrutiny and hoped I didn't have mud clumps in my hair or a weird batch of pimples on the side of my face or something. "How do you know it was a curse?"

I sighed and picked at a hole in my pants. "You're going to think I'm crazy."

"We just watched our teacher sprout fur. How much crazier can you be?" Noah gave me a kind smile that helped to warm me from the inside out.

"Are you sure you should tell him?" Brandon asked from my other side.

He was probably right about keeping my weird powers to myself but after what had happened, I had to explain it to someone. Noah seemed like my best bet at the time.

"I suppose I'm not crazier than you holding a wooden stake up to Caleb's chest." I gave him a look with a raised eyebrow.

"Ah, right." He chuckled. "We can cover that later. Let's focus on one crazy thing at a time."

"Do you know what a Seer is?" I asked, unsure of where to start.

Brandon sighed. "I have a feeling we're both going to regret this."

"I do know what a Seer is. I've suspected you of being one for a while."

"Of course." Brandon folded his arms in his lap and stared as the EMTs loaded Mr. Tyler into the ambulance on a stretcher.

"Well, you're right. I can see ghosts. The one sitting next to me here really doesn't want me to tell you about him." I patted the concrete where Brandon's leg was but of course I didn't make contact.

"That tickles," he grumbled.

Noah leaned over to see the space, and I got a whiff of his body spray. I tried not to get too distracted with how close he was. "I don't see anything, but I believe you. Why doesn't he want me to know about him?"

Brandon glared at the grass. "Because he hasn't earned the right, that's all. Maybe if he stopped hanging around that girl you call a friend. He's just in it for the booty."

I stifled a smile. "He's worried about trusting other people."

"You can trust me," Noah said loudly as if talking to an older, hard-of-hearing person, his eyes staring blankly into the garden beside my porch.

Both Brandon and I laughed.

"It's okay. You can talk normally," I said. "He can hear you fine. He's not an old lady."

Noah sat back, looking slightly embarrassed. "Right. Well, do me a favor and let me know if there are ever ghosts nearby or something. We should develop some secret hand signals."

"We'll get right on that, but you can pretty much assume there's always a ghost around. They're everywhere. Anyway, the point was that he found a cursed chain connecting Mr. Tyler's spirit to some other, far off, something. Somehow, he was able to break it with a ghost pocketknife he'd had in his pocket when he'd died."

I glanced at Brandon for confirmation that I was telling the story correctly.

"Maybe I could break the chain because it had to be done by a ghost. Was the book written by a ghost?" Brandon tipped his mouth to the side as he suggested the idea.

"I don't know. A ghost did give it to me, though. It could be some secret ghost knowledge."

He gave me a side-eye. "Right, because that's a thing."

I shook my head. "I don't know, man. After this week, I have a feeling there's a lot more to the world than just what us humans think we know."

"Fair enough."

"What's he saying?" Noah peeked around my shoulders again as if he'd somehow be able to see Brandon that time.

"He's suggesting that ghosts might be able to handle curses differently, which could have some merit to it."

We had to stop talking about weird things because Trina and my parents walked back towards us after watching the ambulance drive off with Mr. Tyler inside.

"Are you sure you're feeling okay? We could take you to the ER just to be sure." My mom leaned down to study my face some more.

Trina sat next to me on the porch, unknowingly sitting on Brandon's lap.

It was quite difficult to ignore Brandon's grumble about inconsiderate, alive people treating ghosts like trash as he moved off to the side of the porch, his arms crossed over his chest.

"I'm sure. It was the shock of seeing him fall, probably. I am quite a delicate flower." I put a reassuring smile on my face, knowing that it wouldn't be enough to keep my mom from continuing to study me for several days in case I suddenly dropped dead.

Chapter 26

I didn't know what to expect as I walked into history class the next morning. If Mr. Tyler was feeling well enough and had come to school, what did he remember from the curse? It was possible he had been punished for something he did by crossing someone evil and knew about it the whole time, waiting for some brave soul to come along and fix it. Or, maybe even more perhaps, he'd wanted the curse and enjoyed sucking life energy from all the ghosts around him.

Also, I had trouble coming to terms with him being a werewolf and the logical side of my brain wanted to say yesterday hadn't happened at all.

Why was it so much easier for me to believe in ghosts but not in werewolves or vampires for that matter? They weren't that different.

"Hanna!" Noah slid into the desk next to mine. "Are you feeling any better?"

His eagerness unnerved me a little, to be honest, but it was also flattering.

"I'm feeling much better, thank you." I gave him my most confident smile. It helped that what I said was the truth. A good night's rest had restored most of the energy that Mr. Tyler had siphoned from me.

Gran hadn't reappeared, but it hadn't even been twenty-four hours yet. I was holding out hope that she wasn't gone forever.

Noah leaned in closer to whisper, and I could see the flecks of green in his eyes. I decided I liked being this close to him. "Do you know any more about who put the curse on him?"

I shook my head. "I know nothing more than I did last night. I have this terrible feeling that it's going to take some more work to figure out what is going on here. Can you tell me now why you threatened Caleb with a chopstick?"

He sat back in his chair, eyebrows furrowed, and mouth tipped into a small frown. "I'll have you know that Betty is not a chopstick. She's much stronger than that, thank you very much."

"You named your chopstick?"

"She's a stake and a good and sturdy one at that."

"You pointed a stake at Caleb's chest? That's worse than using a chopstick."

He shook his head in amusement. If he was going to say anything, it was interrupted by Mr. Tyler walking into the classroom holding a stack of papers. The tardy bell rang as he set the papers on his desk.

"Good morning, everyone. How was your weekend?"

A few kids spoke, telling him about something totally normal and mundane they had done over the weekend while Noah and I studied Mr. Tyler for any signs of distress or confusion or memory loss. I kept watching him throughout the rest of the period, but he seemed totally fine and himself, as if nothing had happened.

I was beginning to think I had imagined the whole thing.

After Mr. Tyler dismissed class, I worked slowly to pack up my things, giving the other students time to leave before I confronted Mr. Tyler.

Noah took it as a sign that I wanted to talk to him.

"Do you want to talk more about what happened? I feel like our conversation got cut short." He stood next to my desk as I shuffled my notes around, acting like I was getting them ordered properly before putting them away in my bag.

I nodded. "I actually do. I have lots of questions about you, mostly. Especially the ones you don't seem to want to answer. But first, I want to check in with Mr. Tyler to see if he's okay. Meet you at lunch?"

He watched me put everything away and sling my bag over my shoulder. "Are you sure you don't want me to come with you?"

"No, it's okay. I got this. Maybe he'll be more open if it's just me."

He shrugged. "Maybe. See you later."

As all the students left the classroom, I approached Mr. Tyler's desk cautiously. "Mr. Tyler?"

He looked up from his pile of papers with a completely normal greeting smile. "Miss Sanchez. Something on your mind?"

I searched his face for any sign of the events from the evening before. Either he really didn't remember anything, or he was a superb actor. "I wanted to check and make sure you are okay."

"Why wouldn't I be okay?"

I shrugged, trying to convey nonchalance. "Oh, nothing, just heard you went to the hospital last night?"

He puckered his lips in surprise. "Oh, that. Word does travel fast in this high school. It's nothing to worry about, dear. I just had a dizzy spell last night while I was out for a drive. They gave me some fluids and said I was fine to come to work today. Everything feels fine. I'm fine, but if you want to talk more about it, this isn't the place or time. Can you meet me after school by the biology greenhouse?"

Trepidation combined with a need for more answers rippled through me. "Yes. I can do that. I'm glad you're okay."

He smiled and nodded, dismissing me by looking back down at his disheveled pile of papers.

The rest of the day went by smoothly. In fact, it was smoother than any other day I'd had thus far in my high school career. I was grateful because most of the time I was distracted about the events from yesterday, who was what, and my meeting later with Mr. Tyler, hopefully to get more answers.

Noah and I didn't get to talk more about weird things during lunch because all of our friends were clustered at the table. I did notice that Andrea and Noah actually had about an inch of space between them instead of practically sitting on each other. Noah played it cool and acted the same as he always had. I have to say I was impressed by the way he kept up his high-school-boy cover. I didn't quite know what he was, what a necromancer was, or what his connection to ghosts were, but I did know he was something more than just a football player.

All the mundane problems I'd had with high school seemed silly compared to insane things I had learned the night before. Math homework and who sat by who at lunch was trivial compared to who sucked blood and who was hunting late at night on all four legs.

Andrea asked to borrow my homework again and we fell into our old habits easily, without having too much tension between us.

When school ended, after stopping by my locker, I headed outside to wait by the biology greenhouse. Mr. Tyler had probably picked this place because it was usually quiet and deserted. There were classes and clubs that used the inside of the greenhouse, but it was on the far side of the school, away from the parking lot and other places most kids hung out at.

Sunlight warmed my shoulders despite the chilliness of the afternoon. Fall was slowly seeping into the area and the leaves had started turning beautiful colors. I loved listening as the wind rustled the branches and various colored leaves broke free to flutter to the ground, sometimes in groups, sometimes alone.

It wasn't too long before Mr. Tyler approached our meeting spot. He greeted me with a smile, but it felt more genuine than the ones he'd given me after class.

"I'm sorry to have you meet me here. You're probably worried I might try to hurt you again."

"It's okay. I probably should be more scared of you, but we're outside, near a populated area. Plus, the curse is gone, right? You're no longer needing to feed off ghost energy or whatever it's called?" I shifted my bag to a more comfortable place on my shoulder, glad I could still see some students leaving the building in case I needed to call out for help.

I also felt dumb for agreeing to meet him without even a thought to bring a friend. Noah or Caleb would have probably been a good idea, but for some reason, I just hadn't thought about it.

Perhaps Caleb was right to try and warn me to be more careful. Apparently, I wasn't as smart as I thought.

However, Mr. Tyler didn't seem like a predator to me, despite the fangs and fur he could grow. Instead, he seemed more like a victim.

"No." His smile changed to one of grateful relief. "Somehow you guys fixed the curse. I can't believe how much better I feel. Really, words seem trite, but thank you so much."

"Mostly we did it so you wouldn't turn me into a dried-out husk, but you're welcome."

He shook his head and his eyes shone with sincerity. "I was there. You stopped Caleb from killing me, and despite my size and strength, a vamp could take a werewolf mid-change any day. I'd hug you with gratitude, but I don't want you to be any more uncomfortable with me as it is. I imagine all of this stuff might be new to you, even if you are familiar with ghosts."

I chuckled and nodded. "It's all super surreal, honestly. I'm sorry if this is bad manners or something, but after we got rid of your curse yesterday and you almost drained me completely, I don't feel too bad asking, but are you *really* a werewolf?"

He stared out across the parking lot as a few straggling students said goodbye to each other and got into cars. "I don't usually talk about this with students, or anyone outside my pack, really, but I suppose it's too late to hide it. Yes, I am. I change during the full moon when it's easiest, but we can also change, albeit painfully, when we are under threat, which is what happened yesterday."

"But you were able to reverse the change."

"Yes, it's hard to do, but luckily, I'm a bit older than I appear, as young as that is, and I've had many years to gain control. It would have been a disaster to have a fully changed werewolf running around a quiet suburban neighborhood."

I laughed, imagining a wolf scaring my neighbors. "I'm sure it would have been. I'm sorry my friends tried to kill you."

"Oh, no!" He put his hands up in a reassuring gesture. "I totally get it. In fact, if it had been anyone else, I would have agreed with them. Werewolves are nothing to mess around with."

"I saw the claws and teeth trying to come out." My eyes were wide with the memory.

"Exactly."

"Well, I'm glad you didn't terrorize the neighborhood last night and that the curse is gone. Do you think you can tell me a little bit more about the curse? Where did you get it? Why did you get it?"

Mr. Tyler pursed his lips in thought. "It's been a long time, honestly, and some of my memories relating to the incident seem a bit fuzzy. Perhaps that's part of its magic, but I do remember seeing that psychic you brought to banish the ghost before."

"You do? Where did you see her? Why did you guys act like you'd never met before when I introduced her?"

He shrugged. "I couldn't place her exactly and didn't want to make it any more awkward than having a clandestine meeting after school hours to banish a ghost."

I nodded. "I can see that."

"I'm not certain of her involvement with the curse, honestly. All I can say is that she's floating around inside my head as connected to the curse and as one who we should probably avoid."

"Well, that's easy now as it appears she's left town. What things do you remember?"

"Huh, curious. Before the curse, I remember life was going as usual, then some hazy images of a dark night, a stranger dressed in black, a few glimpses of the psychic woman, and then life went back to normal except for I suddenly had a taste for ghostly energy. I didn't even know what it was, at first, just that I needed to be around places that were haunted. Conveniently, my classroom at school had a fairly active ghost. During this last summer, I spent a lot of time at the cemetery and the library. You wouldn't think that ghosts would haunt the library, but I guess they do." He punctuated his sentence with a shrug.

I shook my head with a laugh. "I'm afraid I do know how haunted a library can be."

"Oh, I suppose you would. Again, I'm so sorry about that. I wasn't really myself."

"It's okay. I know it wasn't your fault. If you want to make it up to me, to us, you can help us figure out who did that to you and why."

"I'll try to remember more and do some research. Consider me your personal history researcher!" He puffed out his chest and placed his hands on his hips in a heroic stance.

"Oh, thank you. How long do you think you've been cursed?" I wasn't sure what else to say.

He shrugged. "At least a year?"

"Wow."

"Also, you saved a member of my pack, which by pack rules, means the whole pack owes you a favor just as big. Either we save your life, or the life of someone you love."

"Your pack? How many is that?"

He grinned so big his canines flashed, and while they were still human, they looked sharp. "There are twenty-six of us. Believe me, you want a whole pack of wolves on your side. Especially if you keep hanging out with vampires."

"Right... Well, thank you. I'm sure that will come in handy." I probably didn't appear grateful enough, but I wasn't sure how else to respond. The gravity of his gift was too much for me to understand but I did know that it would be useful, and if the help came at the right moment, it could mean the difference between life and death.

He was still grinning as we said our goodbyes, and I felt like I'd gained another ally. People were coming out all over the place to offer me help. I still wasn't sure I could trust them all or if I could trust any of them, but I had to start somewhere and having a history teacher who was good at research, among other things, might be helpful to have on my side.

Chapter 27

C louds were rolling in the sky as I walked home. The chilly wind cut through my light jacket, and I pulled it closer around my shoulders.

"Hey, glad to see you upright and walking on your own two legs." Brandon stood next to me, popping out of nowhere.

"Holy cow!" I clutched at my chest which had surely just suffered a minor attack. "You've got to warn a girl before doing that! Wait—how are you here? I'm nowhere near the skatepark."

He shrugged. "Remember how I showed up at your house last night? Turns out I can pop in to visit you whenever and wherever you are. Neat, huh?"

Visions of him popping in when I was going to the bathroom or soaping up in the shower made me shudder. "No, it's not neat. We're definitely going to need to set some boundaries."

"Fair enough. So how are you feeling today?" He walked next to me with his hands tucked in the pockets of his giant pants. I will seriously never get over the fact that those used to be fashionable.

"I'm fine. Mr. Tyler seems well, too. We just had a conversation about the whole thing where he confirmed he's a werewolf, thanked me a million times for saving him, which I should extend to you for actually doing the job, and then told me I'd gained the protection of an entire werewolf pack."

Brandon's eyebrows rose and he nodded his head in appreciation. "Wow. Can't beat that. Did he say anything about where the curse came from?"

"He has some vague memories. Apparently, that's part of the curse, to fog up the memory of what happened."

"Helpful."

"Probably to whoever cast the curse, which he did say it had something to do with that psychic, Rose, but he wasn't sure what."

"Yikes. Well, there's another reason why I wanted to talk to you, besides making sure you were okay, of course."

"Of course."

"So, while you were struggling there at the end, as I was sawing at the chain with my pocketknife, I guess my motions created a disturbance of some kind because another ghost showed up, tracing his way to me by the chain."

"Another ghost?" I raised my eyebrows in surprise. "I didn't see anyone else."

"Yes, well, you were totally out of it. Have I mentioned that I'm glad you're feeling better, yet?"

"You might have. Who was the other ghost?"

"I didn't know him and have never seen him before, but he recognized you all hunched over in the grass. He didn't seem happy to see you. He even warned me to stay away from you because you were bad news for ghosts."

I laughed. I couldn't help it. "Me? Bad news for ghosts? How about ghosts being bad news for me? They've plagued me my whole life and now *I'm* bad for *them*?"

"Yes, yes, you're haunted. Boohoo." He waved off my dramatics with a flick of his hand. "I don't know what he meant, but I felt like I ought to tell you."

"What did he look like? Why was he connected to the chain?" I got past my mirth and tried to focus on assessing the situation. Perhaps there was something important going on.

"He looked like a kid from the 70s, probably our age when he died. After he looked at you, he focused back on the chain and asked me what I was doing. After I explained, he told me not to bother and that the curse was tied to a powerful witch whose curses were rarely broken. Then he just popped out like a bubble."

"He—from the 70s? Oh no." I gasped and put a hand to my mouth. "But I thought—"

Brandon looked at me expectantly. "What?"

"Oh crap." I sat down hard on the curb in front of a random house, still two blocks away from my own and put my head into my hands, taking several deep breaths.

Brandon sat next to me and leaned over, trying to catch my gaze. "What's going on?"

"I really messed up. That ghost was in a house that I helped Rose cleanse. I thought we were helping all those ghosts go to the other side. But we were actually..." I looked up and stared out at the street in front of me, tears of exhaustion, fear, and confusion welled up in my eyes. "I guess helping Rose trap spirits. If he was tied to that curse, that means the curse was put there by Rose, or at least she had something to do with it like Mr. Tyler had said. Also, it means that boy, and the several other ghosts, including the teacher ghost, were not sent beyond, but rather enslaved somehow to Rose's wishes. I had started to suspect it wasn't right, but I didn't want to believe it. Perhaps I really *am* bad for ghosts. Especially after what happened to my gran."

The memory of Gran's suffering was enough to send those tears over the edge and I buried my head in my arms again.

"Er—Okay. But you didn't know that's what you were doing, right? Intentions must mean something. Rose used you to get to those ghosts."

"She also used me for my hair, apparently." My voice was muffled by my arms and pants.

"Right, totally normal comment there. I'm sure you'll fill me in on the whole story, but the important part to dwell on is that you weren't doing it on purpose. You didn't hurt your grandma. The curse did. You didn't trap those ghosts. Rose did. Don't be so hard on yourself."

"But without me, they wouldn't have gotten hurt at all!" I wailed into the air and then hid my head again.

Who knows what the neighbors thought of this weird girl sitting on the curb and sobbing to herself, but I couldn't be bothered to worry about my image. There was just too much to process.

"I'm sorry, Hanna. It seems scary now, but it'll work out. We'll fix it. You'll see," Brandon said softly.

"How are we going to do that? She's left town. I don't know where she is, and worse, I don't know what she's capable of."

I felt a soft touch, and I lifted my head, confusion drawing my eyebrows together. Surely, I had imagined the touch, right?

Brandon's hand was resting on my shoulder and both of us looked at it in amazement. His other hand caressed my cheek softly and while it felt as faint as a brush from a butterfly's wings, I could still feel it. His cold finger wiped a tear from my cheek and his eyes met mine. Then, as if worried he'd lose the ability, he leaned in closer.

Our lips met in what was my first kiss and was certain to be unlike any other kiss I'd ever have. It was like breathing in the first snowy air of winter and tingles reverberated throughout my entire body, causing even my toes to wiggle.

It shouldn't have been possible to feel such heat from a ghostly kiss but after getting past the initial contact with his cool lips, warmth as hot as fire scorched through me and I knew my insides were never going to be the same again.

"How did you do that?" I was breathless but not from crying.

A slow, mischievous grin spread across his face as he sat back and pulled his hand off my shoulder. "After realizing you can give extra energy to ghosts, I figured I might use some of it to try and touch you. I know we shouldn't use our own energy or else we could spiral into madness, but I figured it wouldn't hurt if I took some from you. It didn't hurt, did it?"

"Not even a little bit."

Chapter 28

When I finally walked into the house after my longer than usual walk home, Mom and Gran were resting on the couch.

Relief coursed through me at seeing Gran, still a ghost, but whole and not flickering, and I took a deep, cleansing breath.

Then I looked closer at both and noticed something was wrong. My mom's eyes were red and swollen. She even sniffed as I shut the door behind Brandon. Gran was wringing her hands anxiously and looking back and forth between my mom and me.

I gave Gran a quick confused look, but she just shook her head and looked towards my mom, indicating she wanted her to tell me what happened.

I tossed my bag on the floor next to the door and sat down on the other side of my mom, so I didn't sit on Gran. Brandon followed me into the house, but I had all but forgotten him at the sight of my mom's swollen eyes.

"Mom? Are you okay? What's wrong?"

She took a big trembling sigh and used a tissue to wipe at the bottom of her nose. "I'm sorry. I'm not really sure how to say this."

All kinds of terrible ideas flooded my mind. Had there been an accident? Had someone died? My imagination was going so crazy with the possibilities, I almost couldn't stand it.

"Mom?! What happened? Who died?"

She blinked at me, startled. "Oh, no. It's not like that. It's your father. He's left."

"Left?" I glanced at Gran for confirmation who just nodded solemnly.

My mom burst into sobs and her shoulders shook as she cried into her tissue. It was hard to make out her words through the crying. "He packed up and left."

"So, he went on a trip?" I asked, hoping it wasn't as bad as Mom was making it seem.

It was.

"No!" She wailed at the ceiling.

Gran kept shaking her head. "He left for a hotel. She came home early, and he was already home from work, packing up his stuff, trying to leave before her or you girls were home. Then they argued. She threw a plate. It was quite terrifying."

Mom kept sobbing while I listened to Gran.

I rubbed Mom's shoulders and tried to make soothing noises. "Maybe he just needs a break. He could be back soon?"

She shook her head and wailed some more. "I think this is really it. We've been fighting for months. I'm not sure if you've noticed since we've tried to keep it away from you girls, but this really feels like the end."

I had noticed, but perhaps the polite thing to do was pretend I hadn't.

"Oh, you've had lots of fights before. You guys will work it out like you always do."

"You're right. We have had lots of fights!" She sobbed into her tissue.

I looked at Gran and Brandon helplessly. Gran was frowning sadly and still wringing her hands. Brandon looked sympathetic but awkward.

"Maybe I should go..." Brandon edged towards the door, and I did nothing to stop him. It was, after all, a family matter. Plus, I didn't know how to stop him without saying something in front of my mom. He waved with sorrowful eyes and disappeared.

"It'll be okay, Mom. You'll see. I know it seems like a lot right now but try not to think of it all at once. Just take it one minute at a time." I gave her the best advice I had, not realizing I was using the exact words my father had used on me, several times.

And apparently had used on her because she wailed again, and her shoulders shook violently as she sobbed.

I grabbed the tissue box from a nearby end table and shoved it towards her hastily, lest she get snot and tears all over the place.

Because I was so distracted keeping my mom in one piece, it took a while for my own feelings to rise. Part of the pain was seeing my mom like this, while the other part was for the possibility of not seeing my dad very often, if ever. Would he forget about us? He could even go off and make another family and we'd never hear from him again. Would he miss us the way we'll miss him? My mom would have to pay the bills by herself. They could both be gone so much, Trina and I would end up raising ourselves the rest of the way alone.

I didn't let myself burst into tears for fear of causing my mom more heartache, but I'd be lying if I said a few didn't escape my eyes.

Trina came home about an hour later after having gone out with her friends. I hadn't bothered to text her and tell her what was going on at home because I didn't want to ruin her time, give her the news over a text, and figured she'd hear the bad news soon enough.

By that time, Mom had calmed down some. Her eyes were still puffy and red, her fingers still trembled, but at least she wasn't wailing into a tissue, paralyzed on the couch. She'd taken to cleaning the kitchen furiously.

Gran paced throughout the house, going in and out of walls, shaking her head, and muttering to herself occasionally. She probably thought the potential breakup was her fault for not raising her daughter correctly or some such nonsense.

We'd been so distracted, I hadn't even had time to ask her how she was feeling after yesterday's trauma, but she appeared to be the same as she always was, as far as ghosts go.

Trina froze in the doorway as she looked between Mom's furious scrubbing, her puffy eyes, and the mixture of worry and sadness on my face as I sat on the kitchen barstools. I had no idea what else to do or say for my mom, but I couldn't leave her alone, so I'd sat while she'd cleaned.

"What's going on? Did somebody die?"

Mom stood from her cleaning-the-floor crouch and took a deep breath, steeling herself for another conversation about it. She still hadn't told me exactly why he'd left or what they had been fighting about.

"Your father packed up his things earlier and went to a hotel." Mom's lips quivered as she spoke and her voice broke a few times, but at least she hadn't burst into tears again.

I took it as progress.

Trina blinked, looked at me, looked back at Mom, and blinked some more. "What?"

"He's gone, Trina. He's going to look for another place to live and come get more of his stuff when he can." This time, a few tears did leak out of Mom's eyes, and she leaned heavily on the counter to stare out the window.

"What? Why? He can't just pick up and leave like that. He's our dad." Trina kept blinking, as if she were going to clear the pain away and find out all of this was a big joke.

"He's still your dad. He'll always be your dad. He just might be living somewhere else." Mom broke down again and her slumped shoulders shuddered.

Trina beat me to my mom's side and put a soft hand on her back. "It's okay, Mom. We're still here."

Sadness crept into my heart as I watched my sister and mom comfort each other. Gran's worried pacing did nothing to help the mood, and I found that despite my earlier cry on the walk home, I still had tears left inside.

Hours later, after we'd cried and talked and cried some more and tried to figure out what to do next, I was sitting in my bedroom, alone, staring at my phone. Everyone's lives on social media were still the same. People posted the same pictures of themselves having fun or eating or playing with their pets, while my life had completely dissolved into something unrecognizable, in several different ways. It was surreal to look at their pictures and memes while feeling so empty.

Gran fazed through my wall and even though I'd told her that my room was a sacred, no-ghost space, I didn't mind her company then.

"What a terrible evening," she said and sat next to me on my bed.

I nodded, unable to find energy for words I didn't have.

"I come back from who-knows-where to find your mom and dad arguing in the worst way I've ever seen."

Her words reminded me of her disappearance yesterday, something I had somehow forgotten in the drama of the evening.

"Oh, how are you? I'm sorry I haven't asked. I really was worried."

"I feel weak, but I'm alright. I think I'll be fine with time as my energy is restored. How did you get rid of that curse? What happened?"

I told her the story, the short but informative version, and ended it with how Brandon had saved my life without having to hurt Mr. Tyler to do it.

"Brandon does seem like a sweet boy, even for a ghost." We shared a small smile. "So, two other boys came out of nowhere to protect you?"

"I guess. Noah was on his way over to pick me up for our coffee date while Caleb just happened to be in the neighborhood. That's not the weirdest thing about them though, remind me later to tell you how old Caleb is. In fact, he says he knew you."

Her eyebrows raised in surprise and something like alarm flitted through her eyes. "A guy named Caleb said he knew me? Are you sure that's his name?"

"Uh, yes. He's been friends with Trina for years."

Gran frowned and stared at the carpet.

"I'm so glad you're back. I was really worried," I said, wondering if Gran's odd reaction meant that Caleb really had known her.

Gran moved as if to give me a hug but then stopped herself with a sad frown. "I'm sorry you were worried. Speaking of your ghost puppy, part of the reason I came in here was to tell you he's outside in the hallway. He didn't want to rush in here and break your rule, so I told him I'd do it for him and check in on you. He's also here to check on you."

"He's here?" I sighed. "I'm not sure I'm ready for outside visitors."

"He was worried enough to come back here. He could help distract you for a second."

I shrugged, the most approval she was going to get from me.

Smiling, she stood, poked half her body through the wall and into the hallway, apparently telling Brandon it was okay to come inside.

He walked through the door, as if walking through the wall was just too much weirdness for him, and he looked at me with a worried smile and upturned, empathic eyebrows. "How are you doing?"

I shrugged again. It was much easier to shrug than to talk, especially when I wasn't sure what words to use. I didn't have the energy to figure out how I should best act on account of crying myself dry. How does one act after kissing a boy you didn't think you'd ever be able to kiss who also just witnessed your family falling apart?

"I'm sorry your dad left. I can't imagine how terrible you all must feel." Brandon was much better at finding the words than I was.

"Quite terrible, thank you."

Brandon sighed and took his seat in my chair near the desk. "My dad left, too, when I was eight. I'm not sure it's worse or better to have him leave earlier or later in life, but it doesn't matter since comparing won't do any good. All I'm trying to say is that I know it hurts really bad, no matter the circumstances, and I'm here for you, if there is anything I can do, just name it."

I wasn't sure what to say to that, but gratitude seemed appropriate, even if I didn't know what he would be able to do for me. "Thank you."

We sat in silence for a while, each in our own thoughts.

Finally, Gran spoke. "I'm sorry your dad left. I'm sorry you have the burden of seeing the dead. I'm sorry all of this has happened all at once. I know firsthand that trying to help ghosts isn't easy. Some others aren't strong enough to face it and hide away from it for their whole lives. In fact, I tried to do that at one point."

"You did? The way you tell the stories, it seems like you were ready to jump into it your whole life."

Gran chuckled quietly. "I was as scared as anyone else. I appreciate your vote of confidence though. No, I hid behind a necklace for many years, even after the good experience with that dressmaker ghost. I wish I could give it to you now, but I don't have it."

"Oh, right. I remember you saying something about needing to get me a necklace after you found out I could see you. Where did it come from? Can we make another?"

Brandon's back stiffened. "You'd really want to wear something like that?"

"I don't know, but it would be nice to have the chance."

Gran smiled kindly. "It's a family heirloom so I have no idea where it came from or how to make another. We've only needed one of them so far. Perhaps it'll turn up soon."

"Have you heard of a ghost curse that only ghosts can break? Like the one on Mr. Tyler?" I asked, sensing that Brandon did not want to talk about the necklace any longer. I didn't blame him.

Gran shook her head. "I haven't. That whole situation was new to me. I have to admit that there are lots of new things happening to you that I never had to deal with, and all so quickly. It's disconcerting. I fear what this bodes for the rest of your life. If this is the start, what else will you have to deal with?"

Chills tumbled down my spine and I shivered.

"She can handle it. We'll help her." Brandon's smile was resolute and cute.

Gran shook her head. "I don't know how you're going to put up with this one hanging around all the time, but perhaps it wouldn't be so bad to keep him."

"But only just in case another ghost curse comes up." I somehow found a small grin.

"Right," she grinned back, "but only for that reason, because being friends with a ghost is never a good idea."

To be continued...

Don't Bite Vampires

Hanna's story continues in book 2, *Don't Bite Vampires*. Available Now!

Now that Hanna has accepted her powers, she and her ghostly best friend Brandon are ready to help another ghost cross over. When a friend at school admits to not being able to sleep well due to some strange wailing she hears at night, Hanna knows this is the job for her.

That same day, Caleb asks Hanna to contact a poltergeist. This job seems daunting as she is barely coming to terms with her powers—not to mention still struggling with regular high school issues and newly separated parents. Yet, after making a deal with the handsome blood-sucker in exchange for a date for Trina and information on the missing psychic, she agrees to try.

Caleb insists that they must hurry or else his vampire queen will go berserk but calming a poltergeist is no easy task. Even with Gran and Brandon's help, Hanna struggles to get the information they need to prevent a vampire street war that will include human casualties, starting with herself and her family.

About the Author

Jeni Conrad is a wife, mother, teacher, writer, reader, and a human (honest, she can pass those robot tests almost every time!). She usually writes YA fantasy or paranormal stories . Since fifteen years old, she worked in the restaurant business while getting through high school, a BA in English, and then an MA in sociology. Now she works from home while wrangling two small girls, a dog, and two crazy cats.

www.jeniconrad.com

Also By Jeni Conrad

The Lost Guardian Series
Part 1- Game On
Part 2- IRL

The Hanna Sanchez Series
Don't Haunt Ghosts
Don't Bite Vampires
Don't Hunt Werewolves
Don't Summon Necromancers
Don't Hex Witches

The Mirror Islands Series
Peter in Wonderland
Alice in Neverland